AF803390

Bellum

Book I in the BMID Series

George Reaidy

Bellum (Book 1 in BMID Series) by George Reaidy
Copyright © 2021. All rights reserved.

ALL RIGHTS RESERVED: No part of this book may be reproduced, stored, or transmitted, in any form, without the express and prior permission in writing of Pen It! Publications. This book may not be circulated in any form of binding or cover other than that in which it is currently published.

This book is licensed for your personal enjoyment only. All rights are reserved. Pen It! Publications does not grant you rights to resell or distribute this book without prior written consent of both Pen It! Publications and the copyright owner of this book. This book must not be copied, transferred, sold or distributed in any way.

Disclaimer: Neither Pen It! Publications, or our authors will be responsible for repercussions to anyone who utilizes the subject of this book for illegal, immoral or unethical use.

This is a work of fiction. The views expressed herein do not necessarily reflect that of the publisher.

This book or part thereof may not be reproduced in any form, stored in a retrieval system, or transmitted in any form by any means-electronic, mechanical, photocopy, recording or otherwise-without prior written consent of the publisher, except as provided by United States of America copyright law.

Published by Pen It! Publications, LLC
812-371-4128
www.penitpublications.com

ISBN: 978-1-954868-05-2
Edited by Jen Selinsky
Cover Design by Donna Cook

This Book is Dedicated to

@DinzyFinzy *for Support, Motivation, and Inspiration*

Go follow her page:

https://www.facebook.com/authordinzyfinzy

@TheDementedRaven for Inspiration

Table of Contents

Prologue

The decree of the Council was that there cannot be life without order. There must be Balance in the Universe. Good. Evil. Darkness. Light. The Council, which was an ancient body, charged by the Creator Himself to preserve the very fabric of existence, but the Balance had been broken. Earth, now smoldered in ruins, had fallen to the Demon Lords.

Dragan carved a new kingdom amongst his mighty chosen. Some say, the Horseman Bellum, caused the apocalypse and triggered the war that doomed Mankind. But what about the other members, of, the Four? What about Mors? Ila? Discordia? To know those names, one must know another…

The Nephilim is cursed union of Angel and Demon. They put countless of realms to the sword, burnt them to ash, but four of them grew weary of the slaughter. They thought that their conquest would put the Balance in peril. So, a truce was made. The Four would serve the Council in exchange for unimaginable power. Their first task was to purge their brethren from Creation in order to annihilate the Nephilim and destroy their souls.

The myriad worlds of the universe swirl in an endless abyss. The universe was divided into three realms; Heaven for Angels, Hell for Demons, and a third kingdom, Earth, for Mankind. Since the beginning of time, Heaven and Hell had waged wars against each other in an effort to control the third kingdom – to have it for themselves.

Battles raged on the surface of the third kingdom. No one was able to do anything to prevent them, as Heaven and Hell wreaked havoc, leaving behind a shattered and destroyed Earth. Legend mentioned that the Four Horsemen of the Apocalypse were *Mors. Ira. Discordia. Bellum*, the youngest rashest of the four.

Mors, or the pale rider as many called him, had skin as white as snow, with long black hair. He wielded a scythe as his primary weapon. Ila, the only female member of the Four, had long fire red hair, with metal armor from chest to thighs sporting a whip. Discordia, looked more like a human than a Nephilim, with normal soldier armor, as he preferred a traditional dual pistol as a primary weapon.

Bellum wore a red hood covering his long white hair, protected by heavy armor crafted from bones and a steel sword carved with skulls. He scoured the lands in search for Demons to slay and feed his sword. His formidable weapon, *Comedentis*, gave him the ability to steal his enemy's remaining lifespan. Bellum and his brethren were the ones entrusted with the protection of the human race, or so they thought.

To establish peace between Heaven and Hell, the Council forged seven seals from pure gold and tormented souls. The prophecy stated, *Heaven and Hell are finally at peace.* However, if the conflicts arise again and the seals are broken, the Four shall rise to purify Creation from all abomination and protect Mankind.

Bellum, his brothers, and sister obeyed the council. However, they never trusted anyone but each other, for they always had doubt that peace was not permanent. The end of days had come, and the human race had perished while tormented souls were restrained, and living souls were imprisoned in still objects and caskets. Destruction all around, and Earth was lost.

A century had passed since that fateful day, when the Four last cleansed the land and slaughtered their own to save Man. Bellum stood in chains facing the Council accused of rekindling the fire of destruction, causing bloodshed between Angels and Demons, and not abiding by the rules.

But Bellum, convinced that he acted according to the law, pleaded to be sent back to find the one responsible for all this bloodshed and to prove that he was merely caught in the middle of all of this.

The youngest of the Four was on his journey now, to prove his innocence or suffer eternal damnation under the ruling of the Council, but would he accomplish his mission?

Chapter I
Ten Thousand Years Ago

Ursus was born into a cruel and vicious world. A world of kill or be killed, a world where only the strongest would survive. He was the largest carnivore to have ever roamed the land. Extremely robust with powerfully built jaws and very strong claws; they were retractable, allowing them to remain sharp when not in use. Hunting was his favorite sport. Other beings, animals, and anything that carried meat on their bones was appetizing. Anything that moved was, too.

He was a God.

He was the leader of the *Urukana* race, a race of carnivores that weathered Creation to feed on tormented beings left behind by their own flesh and blood. To be a god meant to be immortal, and that was what Ursus was. With every victim taken, he grew stronger and fiercer. Victims, Corpses, Souls, they were all he cared about. That made him what he was. Immortality was just a matter of belief. Ursus, as the leader, was feared by everyone in the tribe. They knew the consequences of not obeying his every desire. He wasn't the typical type of god. He was a killer. What he loved most was destruction, agony, hearing the screams of victims; he was disgusting.

"Why do you slay your kind, Ursus?" an anonymous voice asked.

Ursus didn't know the source of the voice, but he could sense it was a female. It was so gentle and kind as if an Angel was talking to him, "I seek immortality!" Ursus screamed.

"But you cannot be this aggressive, child. You cannot slaughter your own kind. We are related by blood, and every drop wasted is a drop of forgotten memories," she replied.

Ursus was so stunned by the sweetness in her voice, "Angel? Are you an Angel?"

"Angel? What do you mean, boy? We are blood, we are family."

"Angel! You are an Angel!" he shouted. He hated Angels. The conflict between Urukana and Heaven went way back to the time where Ursus's ancestors were searching for a place to call their home more than twenty thousand years ago.

"Why did you come here? Who are you?" the Archangel asked.

"My name is Ura. I'm the leader of the race of Urukana, and we're searching for a place to call home," the Demon bear answered.

"Demons are not welcome in the realm of Angels. Heaven was created only to host those of pure heart and soul. Demons are no such thing."

"Not all demon races are evil, Mr.—"

"The name's Anthrax!"

"Mr. Anthrax, not all Demons are evil. We've been evicted from our homeland and are searching for somewhere to live."

"Leave this realm or suffer the extinction of your race!"

"Wait, please... You don't get it... Please, isn't Heaven about forgiveness?"

"No! We don't forgive what is already condemned."

Ura had no choice but to leave. As he turned his back, the Archangel signaled one of his henchmen to follow the Demon and gather information about his motives. Anthrax turned around and headed back to Heaven as he saw his soldier nod.

As instructed, the soldier followed the Demon as he walked through Eden and reached the outskirts of Heaven. There the Demon met with his people. The look of disappointment on the Urukana race was so strong it could destroy boulders. Before anyone could do anything, they heard a loud thud; the soldier fell from one of the trees as his foot slipped off the branch.

"Sheep, I'm screwed," the soldier whispered to himself. "The Heaven will I do now?"

"YOU! You... You've followed me here! Do you want to kill me? Would you like to carry out the Archangel's threat?"

"No! I—"

Ura left the soldier no time to defend himself as he lunged for an attack, and the Angel soldier had no chance to defend himself. He stabbed himself. Then, he stabbed Ura in the heart and escaped. The Demon bear was left there on the green grass, with Demon's blood spewing out of his heart as he lay there. The story of how an Angel soldier killed the Urukana leader had been passed on from generation to generation, until one of them decided it was time to avenge their glorious leader.

Ursus snapped as his eyes burned with hatred for the being in front of him. Despite unclear vision of who it was, he launched at the source of the voice. Her mouth opened in an attempted to scream for help, but he was her son, her own flesh and blood. How can she save herself and save him at the same time? A sacrifice had to be done. As his mother, she had made her choice.

"Why are you doing this?" She trembled.

Ursus couldn't see clearly who was in front of him because his mind was infected with hatred. "POWER! That's why I'm doing this, for ultimate power! I will take it with my bare hands. All. Of. It!"

Ursus snapped. He slit his victim's throat. The female Demon bear was drowning on the ground in a pool of her own blood.

She stared at her son, on a rampage, and one single tear escaped her eye. "I…forgive you…son."

"Son?" Looking at the body in the pool of blood, he was shocked.

"You are filled with greed. I don't blame you, Ursus. I blame myself for not being there for you the way I should have been."

He stood still, gazing at what his hands had done. "I am not an Angel's son!"

At that moment, his eyes opened; where there was hatred became grief. He had slit his mother's throat. Ursus felt the panic, like a cluster of spark plugs in his abdomen; tension grew on his face and limbs. His breathing became more rapid, shallower. *What have I done?*

"No!" he stood there in disbelief. Nothing he could do to save his soul after what he did. Killing family was the highest form of sin any being could commit.

Ursus fell to his knees, hands on his head, staring at the ground, *I didn't sin*, he thought, as his mother lay dead. *The Four killed their entire species, but they still walk in Creation with unparalleled power! I'll have ultimate power for myself. I'm Ursus. I'm a god!* Before he could lift his face up, The Four appeared in front of him, *Mors, Ila, Discordia, and Bellum.*

"You have sinned, Ursus!" Bellum said.

"You have sinned, too, all four of you! How dare you lecture me about sin!?" Ursus said. "I'll obtain what's rightfully mine and that's power!"

"Power," Mors smirked, his scythe in the form of two smaller blades. "The only thing you are getting, Demon, is a trip to meet the Council!"

"The Council has no power over me, fools! No one can judge me. I do what I want, when I want."

"Is that what you think?"

"I think someone is delusional…" Bellum laughed.

"Maybe he is, but that doesn't hide the fact that he sinned. Punishment is due," Ila said, pointing at the dead body beside Ursus.

"I second that. The Council made the laws for a reason. Balance has to be protected. Sins must be punished!" Discordia said.

"All of you will die! Your powers will be mine! I'm the most powerful of all the Demons, you stupid four, what are you called again, right...They don't have a name for you except Four. Four what? Stupid beings who think that power is earned. It's demanded and executed to the rightful place. I am that place!"

"Stupid?" Ila said, "Who're you calling stupid, Demon?"

"You!" Ursus laughed, "And them."

"Stupid are the actions you've made, and punishment is overdue," they all said unanimously. “Reap the punishment of the evil you have done!”

Ursus wasn’t going to surrender and go with them that easily. He wasn’t the type who gave in, as he lunged at Mors. The attack on the eldest didn’t land because Ila snapped her whip at him cutting both his horns in half. Rage grew inside him. His eyes lit with the fire of a thousand suns combined. Not a single being on the battlefield could understand the reasoning behind Ursus not turning himself in. Instead, he chose the hard way.

He chose to fight! Every attempt Ursus took failed and was in vain; the power of his enemy was even greater than he had ever imagined. Ila and Mors were the only ones retaliating; what would it be like if all members of the Four were to attack at the same time?

Bellum and Discordia couldn’t just stand there watching their brethren fight alone trying to capture the Demon bear. It was time for them to lend a hand, even if the other two didn’t need it. They couldn’t let their brother and sister hog all the fun for themselves. Bellum and Discordia launched their attacks simultaneously as Discordia managed to cut off Ursus's left arm. Bellum scarred the Demon's left eye, and Ursus fainted. When the Demon regained consciousness, he found himself in the presence of the Four along with three unidentified entities–the Council.

“Ursus!"

"I demand to be released; I've done nothing wrong!"

"You have sinned!” the first voice said.

“Sinned, on what ground?" he asked.

“Your mother's blood is on your hands!” the second voice said.

"I know. And, I'm sorry."

"Sorry is only used for mere mortals."

"But I—"

"Our rules are clear, Ursus."

“No, please! You can't be serious! You're accusing me when these infidels did much worse, and you gave them ultimate power! How have I sinned?”

“Peace is worth the sacrifice! You've got no right to judge us! We are the law, and we make the decisions, not you!” the third voice shouted.

"But I am entitled to make my case, am I not?"

"No," the first voice replied.

"But that's unfair. What rule is this? This is not what the Council is about!"

"Ursus, for your treason, you'll be punished and no longer be a god! You'll be stripped from all your powers, from your immortality. Your punishment will be to live on Earth with what's left of the human race!"

"Earth!" Ursus shouted, "That disgusting, filthy race?"

"You are damned to suffer for all eternity."

"Never! I prefer death over living with the humans!" Ursus lifted his blade and charged at the Four.

Mors, being the eldest of the Four, lifted his scythe to the sky as he recited an old imprisonment incantation, *"Siste stultum agere, et flexis sub pedibus nostris petimus misericordiam et formidabunt in ou praesentia. Mori, et posuit in monumento."*

Ila ripped her whip to capture Ursus in a hold he could not escape from.

Discordia used his gun, but the last thing they wanted to do was kill the demon.

While Discordia stood watching the events unfold, Bellum charged at the captured Demon, blade in hand, he recited a spell of his own. *"Sancti lamina meam audiunt vocant, ego praecipio tibi ut restringunt vestra hostiam discite quid maiestatis gustat similis. Restringunt, et accipe quod auferetur."*

The spells were enough to imprison the Demon bear in a soul cage. "I cannot be imprisoned! This is not how this ends!"

"This is what you reaped after killing your own!" Bellum said.

"The law is the law, Demon. You have failed to abide by it! Your punishment is eternal imprisonment," Mors said.

"No! No! No!" Ursus pleaded, "No!!"

The cage Ursus was trapped in began to fade away into the darkest depths of Hell, and his soul imprisoned in an eternal abyss of agony and suffering. He was condemned to relive this tragic moment forever, the moment he slit his mother's throat. The only way Ursus would ever be free was if one of the Four opened the tomb, if blood was sacrificed and a spell binding incantation was repeated.

But was that the last they saw of Ursus?

Chapter II
Present Day

For every good existed an evil to fight it. With so much evil taking over, the Creator had to have a last line of defense, thus the Heaven guard was founded, however Earth was lost! Death, torment, despair, blood, and agony were all that remained on a destroyed surface. Everything was done, over.

Though everything perished to the abyss, the war wasn't even close to its end. On one side Anxo, Heaven's Archangel, blond hair, golden armor and a formidable staff–leading heaven's guards into battle. Alongside him stood his first general and second in command, Alma. Anxo was the leader while Alma stood by his side. Their duty as Angels of Heaven was to protect Man, but having their target annihilated their focus shifted to punishing whoever was responsible for that.

On the other side of the conflict sat Draxus, the king of Demons. The Demon King had no interest in the fight for he knew that his enemies would reach their last breath eventually. He just sat on his throne made from bones and flesh of his fallen victims and his aim was observing the bloodshed.

Was this where Anxo's life got him to? Was this the end of his reign on top of all Heaven's army? Limping on one foot due to injury, holding his right wing, one of the soldiers approached his general in an attempt to convince him to retreat.

"My Lord, we can't keep this fight much longer. They got us pinned down. We have to retreat."

"We have to fight, soldier! It's our duty as protectors of this realm to make sure that evil doesn't prevail here today!"

The injured soldier got down on both knees in a small puddle of blood caused by his injuries, "But my Lord, Hell's armies are smothering us. The men are getting clobbered, and we barely have any left."

"How dare you tell your commander what to do? We aren't cowards! The Creator made heaven and its army to defend everything that's good in this realm! How do you expect us to leave the battle and run away while demons roam freely?"

"But my L…" the soldier tried to defend himself as he looked down to the bloody ground under him waiting for the blade to hit his body.

"My Lord, the soldier is right." Alma interrupted, "We can't keep fighting a losing battle.

Demons are increasing, and we can't call reinforcements. This is not a cowardly surrender. This is to regroup, treat our wounded, and come up with another plan to win this war."

"We don't give up! We're protect—"

"Anxo, the soldier is right! It's not worth losing everyone!"

"Guards! Retreat! Regroup and care for the wounded. We do not leave anyone behind. As for the dead, teleport them back to Heaven where they can have a proper burial. They are heroes, no martyrs."

Any being present there could sense the fear and hesitation in the Archangel's voice, yet they obeyed fearing consequences. Before his lips could even utter that sentence, every being in the war zone felt a tremendous shake in the Earth's core; it was the youngest of the Four, Bellum. No one, mortal, god, or Demon, could believe their eyes.

The prophecy of the Four was about to come true. Were they about to ride again? What would that mean for the living beings in that timeline? Extinction? Annihilation? If the Four rode again, nothing in Creation would be safe from their wrath. Beings who slaughtered their own kind would have no remorse if they were to kill other races, yet the Nephilim race deserved what happened to them.

A Horseman!

Taking a step back, the Archangel thought his mind was playing tricks on him. *A Horseman! That's Bellum! What is he doing here!? How…Is it…? The end…?* More and more questions were left unanswered.

"You cannot be here, Horseman! The last seal was never broken! You are disobeying the pact by being here!"

"I was summoned, Angel! Balance shall be restored as the Four begin cleansing this world!"

"There is no Balance anymore! It died with the last of the previous Four. What's left for you is a realm governed by a selfish Council that can't even protect itself!"

"Silence, insolent fool! The Council is the law, and I am here to make sure the wicked are punished!"

"The only 'wicked' I see here is you, Horseman!" Anxo said. "You are the one who interfered with the events here and betrayed the pact! I don't have the time or the will to argue with you further! Farewell, Bellum!"

"This isn't over, Angel. You will not leave until I'm done with you. How dare you turn your back to one of the Four? How dare you insult the protectors?"

"Horseman! Your brethren are nowhere to be seen! Will you go for this alone?"

"They will be here! You cannot deny the fact that annihilation is near."

Alma couldn't sit there and watch these two argue like children, so she stepped in to interrupt Bellum, "Nephilim! No one is insulting the Four, but you have to look at the facts! Your brothers aren't coming to aid you. You have broken the council's law."

"Lesser beings are not to speak unless addressed!" he said as a look of disgust painted his face.

That was not what Alma was waiting to hear. It made her angry and aggressive, mad, "How dare y-"

"Alma…" Anxo whispered, "Let it go. He doesn't know what is going on, and we intend to leave it that way."

The second in command always obeyed her general, so she stepped back and kept her mouth shut, preventing the situation from getting worse. The Horseman's presence was very intimidating to all the beings in the area. The sense of being paralyzed came to mind. Demons had become vigorous, for everyone knew about the prophecy, about the Four's great powers, who they serve, and what will become of everyone who disobeys the Council. They feared for their lives, yet they were not sure who to fear more; Anxo, Bellum, or Draxus. On one side, they knew disobeying your commander had punishment, yet on the other side, they could only imagine facing one of the Four and what would become of them if they lose the battle. It was like an inception of nightmares.

Did one of the Four carry mercy in his heart? Or whatever the thing keeping him alive was? Would Anxo forgive their disobedience? Was Draxus the demon they should follow?

Nothing made sense to anyone present on the battlefield, yet they couldn't disobey their leader. Punishment for disobedience wouldn't come from Anxo himself, but from the Creator, and they don't want to be part of the Creator's torture. Soldiers began to recover the injured while Alma began her task to teleport the dead back to Heaven.

Could it be a real Horseman! What happened? Who summoned him?

Many questions rose in the head of every soldier on both sides of the fight. Bellum was not amused by the Angel's words. Who the Hell did he think he was to speak to one of the Four? He was nothing, a lesser being, inferior to him. One gaze was all it took to strike fear into the soul of Anxo, Alma, and all the armies of both Heaven and Hell.

"Silence yourself, filth! Who do you think you are talking to? Your slave!?" Bellum answered.

"Nephilim fool! The seventh seal was never broken! You will face judgment! You have sealed your fate by interfering!"

With these few last words, Anxo and all of his army retreated back to the Holy City to regroup, and the Nephilim was left on a shattered Earth. On those streets, he was the only beating heart, the only being of flesh, whatever he was made of. The buildings, or what was left of them, stood in memory of all the victims who fell. They were no vulnerable flesh, but concrete and steel.

The battlefield was bare. Empty. The air was hazy, a red mist thrown up from the sheer blood that was spilt. A fog started rolling over the horizon. It was so thick that Bellum could cut through it. Thoughts went round the Nephilim's head, asking questions about the reason behind all of this. *Why would anyone defy the will of the Council? Who would gain the most from all this bloodshed? All this destruction?*

On the other side of the city Draxus was still on his throne observing the Horseman. The Demon King couldn't just sit there and watch; he always wanted to see one of Them up close and personal, so he stood from his chair and with one leap stood tall in front of Bellum.

"Horseman! It's a surprise seeing you here!"

"Is it, Draxus? Is it!?" Bellum replied.

"Is this the answer I get from the one who executed his own kind to protect a peace that never existed?" the Demon said.

"Peace must be kept, no matter the cost! Or have you forgotten that oath!? You were once one of us. protector of the peace, protector of Man. Then you had to betray your own family, your own *wife* and slaughter your blood and for what? For powers that were and still are not yours? For a chance to be a king of a realm that's already dead? You're nothing but a coward and a murderer, Draxus. Your fate was sealed the moment you held your blade against the innocent! Against your own family!"

"So be it, Bellum! You have sealed yours the moment you held your blade under the Council's will!"

"That was necessary! The Nephilim race put Creation in grave peril. No one, no matter how powerful they are, is allowed to temper with the lives of the innocent! We did what we had to do to save Man and ensure peace is obtained."

"Save Man? Are you insane?" Draxus laughed at the Nephilim's answer, "Man is extinct! What are you fighting for? You and your brethren are like pigeons without a home. You have nothing to fight for anymore."

The Horseman began to get annoyed with small talk and decided the time to act was now, but he had never faced the Demon King in a one on one battle. He seemed shook. He never faced a foe such as Draxus. The Demon King was different; he had long hair that coiled to his filthy shoulders. His gruesome features were covered by what seemed like a large infection, secreting some sort of fluid. His eyes were dark, scintillating pits of madness and horror, his hands jagged claws that dripped fresh blood.

His body was a vile travesty of the demon form. Whatever perverted nature had brought him into being was definitely not in their sane mind. This was a creature from nightmares, a being created in the depths Hell, a creature whose figure could bring screaming madness to the sanest of men.

"Horseman! It's about time I met one of the dreaded Four! Why have you come here? The Seventh Seal was not broken. The prophecy is not yet fulfilled!"

"I heard the call, Demon! I come to purify this land!"

"There was no call! There never was and never will be! The one who summoned us has it! Horseman! You have breached the deal made between your race and the Council."

"Lies! I have been summoned! This realm will be cleansed from you and your evil, fiend!"

"If that is what you wish, Horseman, feel free to jump for the kill." Draxus adjusted his stance.

Though Bellum was known for his kill first ask questions later attitude, he wanted to get more information from the Demon King. That was not the way he wanted to do things, but it was his only option.

"Who sent you, filth!?" Draxus laughed at the Horseman's inquiry. Someone with that immense power cannot even know the one who betrayed them!

"The one who summoned us is amused by your presence, boy! I would love to sit down and chat, but I have some more destruction to deliver and more tragedy to cause! *Be gone!*"

Bellum unleashed a sigh that could destroy mountains. He knew in his mind and in his heart that there was no escape from fighting the Demon King. Knowing he wasn't a match for Draxus, Bellum counted on his stamina and speed to finish the battle as quickly as possible, so he rushed his enemy with a swift attack. Bellum and Draxus danced on a bloody battlefield. The blood oozing from the dead corpses scattered around forced the Nephilim to switch his game plan of swift attacks.

I have to win! I have to protect the humans! Focus, Bellum, focus! Use your full potential your full strength! He thought while swinging his sword left and right. This battle felt unreal. For the first time in thousands of years, the Nephilim could not defeat his enemy. He couldn't land a single blow. *Did I lose everything? Has the Council abandoned me and my brethren!? I knew the Demon King was a formidable force, but not landing a single hit!? Am I destined to lose this battle!? Why?* The Nephilim kept talking to himself all the way through the battle; however, all of his thoughts distracted him from his purpose.

"Horseman! How does it feel!?"

"I haven't lost the battle yet, Demon!" Bellum tried to swing his blade.

"Look at you, trying to be the hero after slaughtering your whole race. Is this what has become of the great Bellum!? You thought you can save a pathetic race such as the humans? You are more delusional than we thought!"

"*We*? Who is we?"

The Demon King never gave his foe the answers he demanded. Instead, he switched form to begin his attack, hoping that the battle would end to his favor, and that was what happened. One swing. One swing of the Hell-blade was all it took to send Bellum into a maze of darkness. Hell, a dark black hole, to some an escape, an escape from the bitter reality they live in. The path of Hell altered beings as they searched for an end, the end of everything. But not all endings end happily.

Bellum was defeated.

What have I done wrong? Do I deserve this death? I am Bellum, one of the Four. I am darkness! I am power! I am immortal! the Nephilim thought.

Suddenly, a voice cracked the silence. "Horseman! Why?"

"Why what? Where am I? What is going on here?"

"You have committed treason, Nephilim," another voice answered.

He couldn't believe his ears, "*Treason?* What are you talking about!? I heard the call! I was summoned!"

Out of nowhere, a third voice, more intimidating than the first two answered, "You have condemned Man to extinction, Horseman!"

"Speak! Who are you?"

"Don't you recognize your creator, Nephilim!?" All three said in unison.

Three sounds! Three distinct voices! Three! How can this be? Am I in Hell? Am I being judged for something I never did? What is going on here? Thoughts started circling inside Bellum's head until his speculations were clarified as the room he was in started to take form. Red was everything he saw. Only red. Walls made of pure glowing magma. Floor eaten by waves of blood. Bones scattered everywhere he looked.

"This cannot be! The Creator can't simply be a ruler in Hell!"

"Who said anything about you being in Hell?" another voice answered.

So, this is true! I am facing the Council! I'm facing treason! I did not kill the human race! "I am not responsible for the massacre! I am not guilty!"

"Horseman! You were the one found on the battlefield! Alone! Solo! Blood all around you and your blade! How can you defend yourself if all the evidence points at you!" all three voices fought back at the Nephilim.

At that moment, Bellum knew he was in the presence of the Council, and entity with no known origin possessing great power. The Council's purpose was to preserve peace between Angels and Demons and to keep Heaven and Hell at bay.

"Send me back! Send me back and I will find out who did this!"

"And if you fail, Horseman?"

"I won't fail! If I do, then the Council should be pleased since their sentence will be carried by someone or something else!"

"Very well, Nephilim, but you will need a weapon! *Comedentis* reeks for the souls of those who perished! Take it and be on your way!"

"Justice shall be enforced! The one responsible will pay with his life!"

Before the Nephilim could leave the scene and start his journey, the strongest of the Council halted him, "Nephilim! You shall leave, on one condition!"

"Condition? Now you put conditions on your warriors?"

"We made you, and we can destroy you! This Watcher will be your burden, Horseman!"

"A Watcher? Why do I need a fucking Watcher?"

"He will make sure that you, Horseman, choose the right side and focus on the bigger picture!" all the three voices replied.

"The Council knows where my loyalty lies!"

"Go, Horseman! Head to the place known as Tidal Crossing! There, you will seek the Demon named Vulgar."

"S, the Council hires Demons now? What happened to staying neutral? To protect every being in Creation?"

"Leave, Horseman! Leave or suffer eternal damnation and slavery!"

"Yes, your Majesties!"

"Don't mock us, Horseman!"

Bellum had no choice but to start his journey where the Council told him, Tidal Crossing. The city was never what Bellum expected. The ghost town was out of place in the rolling hills of yellowing grass. The old road was barely visible. All the destruction ate away the beauty of the area. A gust of dry wind wheezed through the maze of ancient houses where windows had long shattered in the weakness of their structures and rotting boards. Doors hung on the few threads of their hinges and groaned with pain at every sway. Weeds socialized across the cracking asphalt of every road, gathering and laughing at the lone Nephilim as they tried to weave around the catching fingers with every step.

Through the corner of his eye, Bellum saw a strange figure just standing watching him. It was Vulgar; three rows of teeth, each as sharp as a dagger, nose the size of a baked potato, dripping snot, skin a slime green, flaking around the eyes and nose, four protruding eyes, nails like tiger teeth and hands the size of garbage cans.

"Horseman! How can this be? I saw you die by Draxus's hands!"

"Well, I'm back, Demon, and I demand answers!"

"I am but a merchant, Nephilim, how can I be of service? But first may I ask how you got back?"

"That's my business, Vulgar. None of the lesser beings are ever to know! Now, tell me, fiend. Before I fought the Demon King, Anxo said that the seventh seal wasn't broken! Though I was summoned to Earth, the seal remains! Someone has betrayed the peace and doomed mankind!"

"What does that have to do with me? I am but a merchant."

"Don't play dumb! I've known you for thousands of years. Do you even think you are able to fool anyone with your act, especially *me*?"

"I wouldn't dare! I know how formidable the Four are, yet they seek the assistance of a lesser demon?"

"Don't mock me, filth. That smirk will be the last expression your face makes if you do! Now, back to business. I seek revenge on the one who betrayed us! I seek redemption for what's left of my soul!"

"There's no redemption for the wicked, Horseman. You and your brethren set out to exterminate the Nephilim race, yet you brag about the massacre. You brag about power!"

"Anything to preserve the Balance."

"Balance? Balance never existed. Everything is a conspiracy that the Council made up to keep everyone at bay! Do you seriously believe all the crap they feed you?"

"Silence! Never speak nonsense about the protectors of peace! Do you want to lose your life, Demon!?"

"My life has no meaning, Bellum, not since that fateful day when you and your brethren last purged Creation. That day, my race was wiped and I was the only one left alive. I, with other survivors, wish to see you all in agony. As for this moment, I have no choice in what I do since it's all I have. The Council is always watching. How may I be of service?"

"I have to find the traitor! He will pay with his life! I have information that you know who it is!"

"Oh, no, Nephilim, you got this all wrong. I don't have that information, but I know a being who does. Seek the ancient being known as Ursus. His tomb lies at the peak of the highest tower in Tidal Crossing. Unlock his tomb, revive him, and he may be of assistance to a being like you."

"Ursus! We imprisoned him a long time ago! How could he even help me when he knows nothing about what happened?"

"The abyss is but unknown, Horseman. News travels through the silence of the night and the darkness of Hell itself. He knows more than you can ever imagine."

"Very well, Demon. If I find out you betrayed me…"

"I know the consequences of crossing one of the Four. I am neither a fan of you nor of the Council, yet I know my place among you. Head to the tower and free Ursus; he will help you."

"Very well, Demon. Until we meet again," Bellum walked away.

Chapter III
The Journey

Bellum scoured the desolate city alone, searching for what Vulgar talked about, the highest tower in Tidal Crossing, the Tower of Despair. His journey was never going to be easy. Bellum knew what he was getting himself into, yet he ventured on to find the ancient being known as Ursus.

Before any thought could rattle in the Nephilim's mind, he was faced by an evil monster, Grankle. The monster was a predator. He had better vision than any hawk, with jaws as powerful as sharks. He lived in the shadows waiting for his prey to approach him.

For the most part, they didn't even have time to call out and all one could hear was the crunching of bones. The Horseman had no choice but to fight his foe until death, for he knew that any being corrupted against the Council would do anything to prevail and gain ultimate power. The fight seemed endless, choreographed in the midst of bloody streets where victims were beheaded and ripped to pieces.

"Horseman! You have defied the Council by being here! The final seal was never broken!" Grankle said.

"You have no idea what you're talking about, fiend! The Council is the one who sent me to find the one responsible for the extinction of Man. And you, Grankle, are an obstacle in my way! Step aside or face the true power of one of the Four!"

"My master is not a big fan of the Four, Nephilim. He despises you with all his soul. He despises the Council, and he despises every living being not under his command."

"So, be it, monster! I gave you a chance to do what's right. Now, you die!"

"Die? You make me laugh, Horseman! You think death is the end of the road? It's only the beginning!"

"Every beginning has an end, monster. And yours will be by my hand!"

"You? End me? The only being that can "end" me is the being that created me! And that's not you, Nephilim fool!" Grankle lifted his tentacle.

"I won't show any mercy for your soul! You stand against the Council, against the Balance!"

"You still cling to the idea of a Balance that never existed, Horseman! Whereas we, the new order, see the bigger picture where we all live in harmony under the ruling of Dragan! This is true balance!"

"Bigger picture? A world where you become slaves to some abomination? That's what you call Balance? You are delusional! Your fairytale of this new world ends here and now, by my blade!"

"Horseman! Prepare to die!"

It was a battle of life and death. If Bellum survived, he would have answers, but if Grankle was victorious, the Council's sentence would be complete. It was a must win fight for Bellum, yet it wasn't as easy as he thought. The monster had unnatural powers, not like anything he'd ever seen in all the years of fighting. No attack was hitting, not a single scratch.

The Nephilim felt so desperate. First Draxus, now Grankle! How was he to defeat his enemy if his blade couldn't injure the monster? When everything seemed so gloomy?

Bellum heard a gory whisper, "Kill…Feed me…Kill!"

"*Comendentis* is that you? Is that really you?"

"Horseman…Never forget the potential you possess. Feed my anger and gain power like you've never seen before!" the sword replied.

"How will I feed you if I can't even land a single blow?"

"Who said anything about landing hits, Horseman? You forget what the Council gifted you."

"Gifted me? What do you mean, *gifted me*? The only thing they ever done is order me around, as well as ordering my brethren!"

"You forget me, comrade. You forget our connection, the power we possess. Have you put the memories of our battles together aside? All the times when we fought enemies side by side? The Council gave you power, Horseman, they gave you the most formidable weapon, me!"

It seemed like time stopped as those words rumbled the Horseman's mind. It was like he had an epiphany, a vision.

"Bellum, our gift to you is this blade. It has the power to steal your enemy's remaining lifespan, as well as obeying your every command and make your thoughts a reality. Use it wisely."

The young Nephilim couldn't believe his ears or his eyes, he was finally one of them, one of the Four, and with a powerful sword like the one presented to him, he will protect Creation until his death. Although excited and ready for battle, the Horseman had doubts about the real purpose behind the blade he now wielded.

"Why have I been chosen to wield this blade?" he asked as he gazed upon Comedentis for the first time.

"Your brethren each have a unique weapon that complements their character; Mors has the scythe, Ila the whip, and Discordia the pistol. Each one of the holy weapons has its own features that are suitable only for the one carrying them."

"What if I wasn't deemed worthy?"

"The weapon chooses the master, young one. Comedentis chose you for a reason."

What does this blade see in me? I am but a mere child wielding a sword. Who knows when I'll get injured using it, or even die? I cannot do this. I want to be one of the Four; this is my dream. But this doubt, those thoughts, what if I'm not good enough?

Hesitation and confusion ran around in the Nephilim's mind until his thought sequence was broken by a mysterious voice, "Kid…Do you doubt yourself? Aren't you the great Bellum, the strongest of your brethren and keeper of peace?"

"I am! I am one of the Four! I am the protector of Man, protector of the Balance!"

"My power comes from within your soul, Nephilim, and through your mind and spiritual energy. Focus! Focus and defeat any enemy you face!"

The Nephilim found himself, yet again, standing in the presence of Grankle who tried another attack in hope of finishing his enemy off. With the blade in hand, he stood firmly in his ground waiting for his foe to get closer to unleash his attack. As soon as the monster got to a few feet from Bellum, the Horseman swung his blade when black smoke emerged and cut Grankle in half from top to bottom.

The fight was over. Bellum stood there watching the fiend's corpse fade away as a door behind it opened, the entrance to the tower. The Nephilim ran up the stairs where he reached the top. It wasn't what he expected. The sun seemed so bright yet so dim at the same time, drifting away in the sky towards the mountains reminding Bellum of another day gone by. Bellum stood there admiring the beauty of the tower, gargoyles everywhere made of pure gold and red fluid as if blood was dripping. On the ground were narrow tunnels that stretched from each gargoyle to Ursus's resting place.

"How am I supposed to revive him?"

"Horseman, you remember the spell, don't you?"

"Of course, filth! Do you question me!?" Bellum looked around maybe he'd find another clue as to how to revive the ancient one. He had no choice but to try his luck, so he recited the incantation, "*Audire me dicere, Daemon. Surge et sta coram me in conspectu tuo magister et imperator. Audire me voca, et veni, porro ex profundo Inferni et obedire.*"

"Nothing happened, how can this be!? This is the spell! I am sure of it!"

"There's something missing, Horseman. Do you remember what the Council said when they imprisoned Ursus? The only way to free Ursus is if a blood sacrifice was made and the spell recited."

"Yes, indeed, a blood sacrifice!" Bellum cheered. He looked around and spotted the liquid dripping from the statues around the tomb. As he approached one of them, he extended his hand to the liquid touching it, then tasting, "This is blood! This is the sacrifice!"

One by one, Bellum turned the statues to face the tomb. The tunnels on the ground turned red, as well as the tomb.

"Now, Horseman, recite the spell again!"

"I don't take orders from filth! Keep quiet! *Audire me dicere, Daemon. Surge et sta coram me in conspectu tuo magister et imperator. Audire me voca, et veni, porro ex profundo Inferni et obedire.*"

The tomb glowed with a red light that engulfed the top of the tower and blinded the Nephilim and his watcher. The tomb opened. When the blinding light was over, Bellum saw the ancient one known as Ursus standing in front of him holding his blade in his right hand. Before any word was spoken, the demon bear charged Bellum with an intent to kill him.

"I won't fight you, Ursus!"

"Good! Then, killing you will be easy. Next, it'll be your brethren!"

"You don't want this! Trust me! I am here to help you."

"Help me!? Ten Thousand years, you *bastard*! I was imprisoned because of you, your brethren, and your stupid Council! Is this what you call help?"

"That was necessary! You slaughtered your own family in cold blood! If we hadn't imprisoned you, all of Creation would've fallen by your hand! Do you really think the Council would accept that!?"

"I don't care what the Council thinks! I don't care what you think! I wanted what you have, all four of you! I won't rest until I have it!"

"If so, then quit thinking about vengeance! This will lead you nowhere!"

"HELP!? You think I will help you after everything you did to me? I owe you nothing but a beating for the pain and suffering you all caused me!"

"I do not have time to argue, Demon! Do you want your full power back? Do you want everything that was taken away from you?"

Power was what he really wanted, to be like the Four, immortal again. Despite what he wanted, Ursus had doubts about the Horseman's intentions. He trusted no other being but himself, yet one of the

Four offered assistance. *How could he refuse? But what if he was lying? What if he was sent here to kill the ancient Demon?*

"How do I know I can trust you, Horseman?"

"To begin with, I freed you. Second, if I wanted you dead, I would have killed you already. Am I not capable of killing a mortal?"

"You've got a point there. Speak!"

"Ancient one, I need your help. The worl—"

"The world crumbles under the reign of Dragan, Horseman. You rode to the third kingdom when no call was given, when the last seal wasn't broken. You have been accused of treason and you seek redemption."

Surprised to hear the truth for once, Bellum stepped forward, "You know this how, demon?"

"Nephilim, I'm sure you've heard that the abyss knows all; every event, every action, and every soul giver or taken passes through the abyss."

"I need to redeem my—" Bellum tried to say when he was interrupted again.

"Redeem yourself, your name, and your brethren."

"Yes! It's the purpose that drives my anger and fuels my rage!"

"Horseman, rage will solve nothing. What you need is to focus your strength where it really needs to be. I will help you, Nephilim, but before I do I have some doubts."

"Doubts!? Even after I freed you!?"

"Yes, Horseman. I will help you, but tell me first what's the catch! You, who do the Council's biddings, don't offer shit unless it serves in your favor!" Ursus sat down on one of the statues around his tomb, "You surely know that the Council has a hand in all this chaos, don't you?"

"The Council was the one who sent be back here to find the traitor! How could they be in on this!?"

"The Council loves power too, Nephilim. Do you think they gave you power just because you wanted peace? Because you were tired of fighting? You are so delusional, Bellum. The Council did what they did to ensure that they stay in control of Creation and every being in it. That's why they send the Four to finish their messy business."

"They are responsible for the peace between heaven and hell! The keep the Balance and peace!"

"Balance? Are you insane!? There was no Balance to begin with! The Nephilim were the ones responsible for annihilating almost all other races and tribes. It wasn't favorable for the Council to watch Creation get destroyed. That's why the created the Four, to stay on top of everything, in control!"

"He's not to be trusted! I can feel that he is planning something big!" the watcher interfered with a trembling voice.

"Filth! I said I have no choice! He's the only one who knows where Dragan's tower resides. He is the only one able to take me there! I need to get there by any means."

"You know betrayal is Ursus's middle name."

"If he ever tries to even lift his blade, he's dead. And he knows it. That's how I'm certain his loyalty resides with me. Once he opens the portal and leads me to the Angel of Despair you can consider him as good as dead. I need to find Dragan and stop his reign of tyranny!"

"Horseman…The only blade that can damage Dragan is the Blade of Eternals. As for the true identity of Dragan and his whereabouts, the only being capable of helping you lies inside the Tower of Hope where Shaman, the Angel of Despair, is trapped. However, I cannot open the portal to the tower just yet. I can help you, but I need you to help me first."

"What is it you desire, ancient one?"

"You remember ten thousand years ago when you and your brethren imprisoned me and took away all of my power? I want it back."

"You can't begin to imagine how hilarious your request is. Can you, Demon?"

"I know what I say sounds ridiculous to you, Nephilim, but if you ever want to get to Shaman, you will restore my power. Without them, I cannot help you."

"How do I know I can trust you now, Demon?"

"You don't have to, Horseman. As a sign of faith I will grant you something the Council hid from you and your brethren. Do you remember how you used to be fearless, doubtless, heartless, and a savage killer with no conscience?"

"That was a long time ago, fiend. I'm not that being anymore."

"To defeat Dragan, you've got to tap to that energy again and return to your former self. The only way to help you is by forcing it into you." Ursus raised his blade to the sky and began mumbling inaudible words, "*Audi me, et veni de aliis antiquis virtus immortalitatis. Vocem meam audiunt, et egredietur de tenebris et faciem tuam hostem*"

"What have you done, Ursus?" Bellum felt the pressure of a thousand rocks upon his head.

"It is the only way, Horseman! You have to tap into your hidden source of power! I have released your former spirit energy that the Council erased from your memory. With this power, you are able to contest with the strongest of beings."

Bellum could feel himself different, he looked different, too. The white hair disappeared and was replaced by red blood shorter hair while his armor switched from white to a resounding dark purple. "The only way I can open the portal is by regaining my full strength, my full potential. Remember all those years ago when you and your brethren judged me? You took my power and divided it among four chosen ones to help keep it away from me if I ever came back. Find those chosen ones and bring me their still-beating hearts. And I think I made myself a little bit more trustworthy in your eyes, have I not, Horseman?"

"For the time being, yes."

"I cannot open the portal unless I have my full power, Bellum! Remember that."

"I know I will regret it, but I will help you ancient one!" Bellum replied.

"Very well, Nephilim. The first of the Chosen resides in the Cathedral. The first of the Chosen is Onyc, the Bat King. To get to the Cathedral, you must traverse the Desolate Grounds. Be very careful, Nephilim, for the path you are going to take isn't bare of enemies. The road is infested with tormented souls, not to mention the army of Heaven."

"The forces of heaven, you say? Since our first encounter I wanted a piece of Anxo and his feathered friends. Seems that this quest will be fun after all."

"Before you go, Nephilim, you need to hear this."

"Hear what, ancient one?"

"The only weapon capable of competing with Dragan is the Blade of Eternals."

Bellum was surprised, yet he figured that might be the only way. Last he knew about the blade was that Shaman had it.

"Horseman…The blade was split into three pieces each hidden in a different part of Creation. If what the tormented souls are saying is true, you will find them on your journey to slay the Chosen ones."

"How can it be that it's broken into all those pieces and scattered around?" Bellum asked.

"The Council saw that the blade was such a powerful weapon for one person to handle. As such, they asked the Angel of Despair to relinquish it so it can be hidden properly, but he refused. The Council took it upon themselves to take it by force, break it, and scatter it around Creation so that the Chosen help protect it as well. Shaman was imprisoned in this process. As you venture to collect the hearts, you will find the pieces."

"Very well, fiend. Enough wasting time, I will be on my way now."

"One more thing, Bellum."

"Stop wasting my time!" Before Bellum and his comrade took another step, they got a few final words from Ursus, "Nephilim…Seek the Holy Hammer. You will find it very helpful on your journey of redemption."

"Wait. The Hammer? And you mention this *now*? What the fuck is a holy hammer!?" the watcher screamed.

"Peasant," Bellum whispered, "I know what he's talking about. The Hammer is said to be a powerful weapon capable of slaying armies with a single blow." Bellum shifted his sight towards Ursus, "Very well, Demon. If you have no more words for me, I'll on my way."

"Go, Horseman! Return the heart of the Bat King, and you will be rewarded," Fatigue was his challenger now. Neither Nephilim nor watcher could resist the urge for a good sleep, so that was exactly what they did. Bellum opened his eyes. In the dark stillness, he couldn't see much, but the dim glow of a torch and the vague shadow of a figure next to it. Half asleep, he fumbled and checked his reflection in the water.

With a massive headache from the experience he went through, he searched the area where he slept but couldn’t find a single clue to his whereabouts. Washing his face, he took a glance at the torch in the distance, and waited. After his eyes adjusted, he knew that he wasn't in the tower where he freed Ursus.

Chapter IV
The Hammer

As Bellum walked farther into the forest, he heard creaking sounds. Even though it was eerie, his curiosity got the best of him as he walked toward the sound. When he arrived at the spot where the sound was emanating from, he saw what appeared to be a girl's figure; it was Raven. It became visible that the girl was on a wooden bench, eating what seemed to be a cooked rat. The girl had stringy auburn hair that went past her shoulders. She wore flak from top to bottom colored in red, vibrant red. She had a muscular body, one that you see on gladiators.

The girl didn't even notice the Nephilim when he got closer to her. When opening his mouth, he started to choke on the thick air. After what seemed to be years of him standing there, she finally became aware of his presence. When they made eye contact, she cocked her head to the side like she was taunting him. Something about her told Bellum that she knew more than her silence gave away. Her eyes were blue as the sky in broad daylight. They looked as though they were full of hope.

She was no ordinary girl. Her spirit energy was nothing like Bellum had ever felt before, so radiant and powerful. While Bellum stared at her, she was examining her companion as if she was looking for something. Her gaze was so staggering it felt as if she was staring into Bellum's soul. She sat there minding her own business eating the food she hunted earlier that evening.

"Is that a rat you're eating, kid?" Bellum asked.

"Who ye callin' kid, mister? I am more than ten thousand years old!"

"Ten thousand years old? With that appearance? Who are you fooling, kid?"

"I said don't call me kid! The name's Raven!"

"Okay...Raven."

"And, ye are?" The girl stood up.

Bellum took a step towards her trying to grab her arm, "Do you not recognize me, woman?

The little girl snatched her arm away, lifting her blade with the other as she went for a swing, "Aye. Ye are Bellum. Ye are one of the dreaded Four."

The Nephilim was intrigued. She knew him, yet she held her blade against him.

"If you know, why hold your blade against me, young one?"

"Ye tried to hurt me. It's natural that I try to defend myself."

The Nephilim was astonished to see that such young being was able to fight. "Who taught you how to hold a sword and fight?"

"Paps."

"Well that's a vague answer. Could you tell me his name?"

"Jynn Wallace Sakhai," She drank from the flask next to her.

The Horseman couldn't believe his ears. That name…He knew that name. Could she be who he thought she was? Daughter of the one and only Jynn Sakhai, the Maker? What Bellum remembered about that race was that they were annihilated when the first Four cleansed the land millennia ago. Could she be the only survivor?

A Maker!

There was something wrong in the area, but he couldn't quite tell what it was. The atmosphere was dense and strange, though apparently invisible to his eyes. What the Four and what the Council knew about the Makers is that their race was extinct when the Four first rode to cleanse Creation from evil. The Maker tribe, as well as the Anaiim race was cleansed a long time ago. They were accused, wrongfully so, of forging the Abomination weapons and supplying them to the forces of Hell to take over Creation.

How is she here? My ancestors killed her race to the very last living breathing soul. How is it possible that she lives? How can this be? Did the Council lie to us? Were the Makers wrongfully accused of the sin they carried? Why would they not defend themselves if they were innocent? Bellum thought.

As he looked at the girl, he could notice she wasn't in total focus to what was going on around her.

"Raven…" a tender voice said, "You have to leave, little one."

The young Maker was confused as to where the sound was coming from, so she didn't know how to react; she remained as still as a rock.

"Raven…" the voice said again, "You have to run. They are coming."

"What? Who's coming? Who's here?"

"Run my child!"

"Mother? Is that you?" Raven's eyes filled up with tears, "What's happening? Who's coming? What…"

"There's no time to tell you the whole story, little one, but whatever you hear or see as you grow up, always know that mommy and daddy will love you forever."

"Mother, I can't leave you!"

"Run! *Run before they come to get you. We have been accused of treason and the Four are coming to punish the whole tribe. You have to survive and carry our legacy." The woman coughed blood on her daughter's dress.*

"I won't leave! I won't r—" Raven cried as a figure appeared over her body. It looked like a muscular being with a big sword carved with what seemed to have the form of engraved heads. Raven couldn't see clearly who that thing was, but she got up and started running, just as her mother told her. As she ran with tears in her eyes, she took a final look back at home to see the being swing his blade and murdering her mother.

"I remember ye…Ye are the being that slaughtered my mother…without remorse…"

"I had done no such thing!" I only began my duty as one of the Four a few thousand years ago. When were they murdered?"

"Thousands of years ago. We were just living in peace when the Four arrived and killed everyone. I was lucky my mother helped me escape before that sword you wield, stabbed her heart, and killed her."

"The information that we have dictates that the Makers were making weapons for the demons to use and take over Creation. To save what was left, the Council ordered our ancestors to cleanse the race to prevent the destruction of Creation. Preserving the Balance was necessary."

"At what cost, you boggin bampot?" she lunged herself with an attack. She could care less about consequences. She wanted revenge from the being who killed her mother. She had her suspicions when she first saw him, but what made her thoughts reality was the mere sight of his blade.

"You do not want to do this, child!"

"Silence, ye doaty creature! Ye were responsible for Ma's death! Ye pay for that!"

"Kid! What happened couldn't be undone! I am sorry for your parents. I lost my family, as well!"

"Ye chose to slaughter yer own to gain power!" the girl screamed and cried as she got on her knees, "It was a choice! I had nothing! I had to watch Ma die by that sword, and for what? Balance that never existed? For a false accusation?"

"Kid…I cannot take back what my brethren and I did all those years ago, but at this moment I need your help. A greater evil is threatening everything we worked for, the peace that we protected for a thousand years."

"Yer bum's oot the windae! Ye think you're getting help from *me*? Yer more of a numpty than I ever thought!"

"I am sorry, kid." The Horseman kneeled next to her and gave her a hug. "I am sorry, little one. I know we can't bring them back, but I promise that I'll always be here when you need me."

Raven was so confused. *How could one of the Four be so kind and gentle? Was he playing her? He wasn't to be trusted! His ancestors slaughtered her tribe! He must die!* She thought she could be a fair opponent to one of the Four, yet what she didn't know was that Bellum was the best swordsman among his brethren. With a single dodge, he could repel Raven's attack and land one of his own. The aftermath of that short battle was Raven sitting in a pool of her own blood after the Nephilim cut off her arm.

"Why would you even go for an attack, kid!?" Bellum asked.

"Revenge!"

You can trust me, kid." Bellum held his blade close to her detached limb. "*Potens potentia, audi me, et resurgent, quae capta.*" As he recited his incantation, he placed the tip of his blade over Raven's cut arm.

She couldn't believe her eyes. Her arm was restored; she had two hands, *again.*

"Do you believe me now, Raven? I regret all the massacres my ancestors took part in and I want to make everything right again."

"Let's say I believe ye for a moment. What do ye want, Nephilim?"

"The Holy Hammer…is the wea—"

"Ye want it…" Raven replied knowing where the Nephilim was going with his words.

"It is the most powerful weapon after the Blade of Eternals capable of—"

"The Hammer cannot kill whoever yer after, Nephilim. It's just a tool to get to where ye wanna go."

"A tool? But Ursus said it's the most formidable weapon ever created, second to the Blade of Eternals."

"A tool, Horseman. Follow me." Raven started walking toward a thick fog at the edge of the forest.

Bellum had no choice but to follow a little child to wherever she was taking him. *Was she taking him to his doom? To help him? Where?*

After what felt like an eternity of walking to the unknown, Bellum and Raven arrived at a secluded portion of the forest surrounded by tall trees all carrying blood red leaves. In the center of the forest, a weapon, firmly pushed to the ground, stood.

"Ye wanted the Hammer..." Raven pointed towards the center piece, "There's your Hammer stuck in the ground over there. Let me remind ye, Nephilim, the Hammer is just a tool."

"The Hammer!" Bellum had a big smile decorating his emotionless face, "Finally, I can get the job done!"

"Try to pick it up."

Bellum approached the planted weapon, hoping he could be the new wielder. However, his mind wasn't there with him. *Was this a trap? Would she be that smart to plot a trap for any newcomer seeking this formidable weapon?* Though his thoughts killed his enthusiasm, he still went for the blade. As he wrapped his hands around the handle, he could sense a gravitational pull taking his body; he couldn't pull the weapon out of the ground.

"What? How..." Bellum asked.

"I told ye, Bellum. The Hammer isn't some weapon ye find and use. It is a tool, and like any other holy weapon, it chooses the wielder."

Raven stood by his side with a big smile on her face as she extended her hand and lifted the Hammer with ease.

"The wielder is you then. I see now. You are the Holy Hammer…The most powerful weapon in all of Creation, is a child?"

Raven wasn't amused with the Nephilim's words, "Ye asked for ma help, Lavvy heid. If ye still want it, let's go."

"I need to defeat Dragan. The Council guided me to Ursus, but he needs the hearts of the Chosen ones to get his powers restored. Only then he will help me."

"Ursus isn't to be trusted and ye know that, Nephilim."

"I've been hearing the same sentence over and over again. I know I can't trust the Demon bear, but

I have no choice in this matter, for he is the only one who knows where Shaman is."

"Shaman ye say? He resides in the Tower of Hope, yet the ancient one is the only being who can open a portal and get you there. Let's focus on one task at a time, Bellum. Can I call ye Bellum?"

"That would be nice, kid."

"Okay, Bellum, let's go get the first Chosen. What can ye tell me about it?"

"He's Onyc the Bat King, and he resides in the Cathedral."

"Ah, yes, the Cathedral. This way, Horseman. This will be a five-day journey unless you can fly there, then it's faster, a lot faster."

As they walked through the forest, unanswered questions haunted the Horseman. *How did this child attain this much power? Was it because she was traumatized during her childhood, she unlocked a secret ability to wield a powerful weapon? Why her?* All along the road, Bellum couldn't stop wondering about this little girl. A Maker with immense power, now that was something else.

"Bellum, we meet again!" a voice from the sky above could be heard.

"Anxo! How did you know about my whereabouts?" Bellum asked.

"You are not a hard being to track, Horseman. We always knew the path you'll take. You seek

Shaman, so I figured that the Hammer would be your first go-to task." The Archangel looked toward Raven, "Girl…Do you know the being who stands before you?"

"Bellum, one of the Four!"

"And do you know that it was the Four who were responsible for your race's annihilation? How can you stand as his ally when his race was responsible for the massacre that killed your family?"

"Shut yer pus, Anxo. If yer here to kill my friend here, then ye have something coming at ye, gowk hackit!"

"Friend?" Alma laughed loudly at what Raven said, "A friend who killed her family. He must have brainwashed you. Poor little kid."

"Bellum isn't like his ancestors! He restored my limb! He helped me contain the grief and focus on the task at hand! He is a good Nephilim."

"There is no such thing as a good Nephilim, silly little girl. Nephilim annihilated races and tribes, and clans and brought civilizations to the ground for what they call the greater good! Nephilim will always be the enemy! Now and forever!"

"You were lucky the last time we met, Angel, but now luck isn't on your side," Bellum threatened.

"Lucky!? What you call luck I call smart, Nephilim. You were the luck one at that time because we refrained from attacking. With this army, you will never see tomorrow's sunrise!"

"Refrain from your threats, peasant! You are no match for one of the Four. Not even your army is."

"Might as well, Horseman. The time for talk is over!" Anxo lifted his sword, "Today will be your last day among the living, Horseman, and this forest will be your graveyard!"

Raven was fed up with all the talking and threatening, so she stood in front of the Horseman holding her Hammer over one shoulder and a sword in the other. As Anxo gave the order to attack, Raven smashed her sword firmly into the ground and held the Hammer is both hands mumbling to herself, "*Malleus Ego Praecipio Tibi! Concede Mihi, Tua Plenam Potestatem Perdere Inimicum*" were the words her father taught her when she was just a mere child, a couple centuries old. The spell she blasted was enough to awaken the full power of the formidable weapon she held in her hands, and with that power the entire army of Angels fell down, except for Anxo and Alma.

"This cannot be! How could a mere child slaughter an entire army of powerful guards?"

"This is the power of the Holy Hammer! Any of ye want to fight anymore? I will blast yer ass back to heaven. Suck on ma baffies ya wee bairn!"

"She is the Hammer! Her powers are far greater than both of you combined. I suggest that you get back to where you came from before she changes her mind."

"Is that a threat, Horseman?"

"If you know what's best for you, you will turn around and head back to heaven where you belong."

"How dare you order an Angel around, Nephilim? You will pay the price of your insolence with your life!" the second in command flew down in an attempt at the Horseman.

"*Alma*! *Stop*! Don't do this!"

"They have slaughtered our family! *Our friends*! They will perish!" she launched an attack on Bellum, "You wanted him dead some time ago and now you want to spare his life? How can you do this?"

"His life is a necessity now! Do you want to face the wrath of the Council when they find out it was an Angel who killed one of their servants? Do you really think that they will keep his death in wraps? Think about your home, our home. Think about all the ones still alive there. Do you want to see them dead? You know what the Council is capable of. Do not go forth with your foolish act!"

The second in command was blinded by hate and disgust as she kept on attacking the Horseman fearlessly. No matter what the consequences were, she had to fulfill her oath to herself. She had to kill Bellum. That was her only purpose after the massacre minutes ago.

"Alma! I don't want to fight you..." Bellum began dodging the general's attacks, "We are allies. We fight to protect Man and the peace between all beings in Creation. You do not want to do this!"

"What do you know about protecting Man? You are single-handedly responsible for the extinction of their race! You protect a Balance that the Council created. As for us, we protect our own! You have no right to talk to me about protecting the innocent!"

"That wasn't me! I was set up! The Council sent me back here to find out who was responsible for this massacre! I regret the death of your friends here today, but in our defense, you attacked first and we had to defend ourselves."

"You will never leave here alive, Bellum! I will kill you! I will end your very existence and have Creation rejoice to your death! No more purging. No more cleansing. We will live together without the fear that anyone might trigger the apocalypse! Our race will be protected!"

Swords grinded in a fierce, yet beautiful, dance of destruction. Anxo and Raven just stood there amused by the fight, they were amused by what they saw. A Nephilim, one of the Four, against the strongest Angel after Anxo himself, fighting for something as heinous as pride and honor in a world where power rules over the weak.

Why would they even try to stop them? Both Anxo and Raven wanted Bellum dead deep down in their hearts, each for their own reasons; Anxo to overthrow the Council without having one of the Four against him and Raven as revenge for killing her mother. Alma, being a creature who enjoys winning, thought of turning things around to her favor, so she called upon her steed, a Griffin in an attempt to distract the Horseman.

Bellum saw everything coming; the fight, the griffin, the way to Onyc, the first of the Chosen, and his ticket out of the forest. As Alma rode her mount, Bellum threw his blade toward the beast aiming for the griffin's wing, yet he managed to hit the Angel and cut her wings, throwing her off her steed. Without hesitation, the Nephilim grabbed his sword and then the beast by its neck, rode it and flew away heading to his next destination, the Cathedral, leaving behind his one ally, Raven.

Chapter V
The Cathedral

Bellum rode the beast until he reached the entrance of the sacred cathedral, Onyc's nest. As soon as the griffin reached the cathedral, Onyc launched a surprise attack on the unwanted guests. The flying beast took the Nephilim's transportation and threw the rider to the ground, and left it fighting with the other flying beast. The Nephilim stood up with intent to kill the bat instantly.

However, the Watcher got in his way, "So that's Onyc…Not so magnificent as we thought!"

"We have a mission, fiend, the heart of the Chosen."

"We do, Horseman. But the question remains. How are you going to fight a flyer with nothing to get you close to it?"

"You got a point there, watcher."

For the first time since he became the Nephilim's burden, the watcher made a good point when he opened his mouth, "Nephilim, there!" The watcher pointed to a chain ladder on the side of the entrance.

As they approached the cathedral, they were amazed by the location. It was a complete mess, to put it nicely. From outside the boarded windows, the paneling and the door that was bolted with iron rods, all looked scary and threatening enough to keep the limited number of visitors away.

However, behind the scary exterior the interior was equally destroyed, if not worse. There were no doors separating the rooms on the ground floor, yet they could be found a few feet into each room often with large chunks torn out of them, large scratch marks. Most of the furniture had survived with minimal damage, only a few scratches and chips to their name. There was only one staircase leading to the other floors, where the Horseman found the same marks on the walls and furniture. The only light source for the dank, dark building was the cracks within the roof and barricades over the windows.

Bellum made his way up the damaged stairs. As expected, no other living being lived inside the abandoned cathedral, or maybe the bat monster devoured what resided once. *How else would a carnivore feed himself?* There was no doubt that whatever lived here was now gone.

His footsteps echoed throughout the empty halls. The light entering from the cracks lit his way as he continued the search for a way up to the roof. The Nephilim kept walking, not getting anywhere. The barrenness of the whole thing sat on his shoulders, an unnecessary pressure. He shuddered with the overhanging dampness and pressed forward through the murky hall until he finally reached the roof.

As Bellum reached the roof, he could see the griffin he took still fighting with Onyc. Bites and claw attacks were the only way for the griffin to protect itself from an angry Bat King. Ruthless and cunning, the bat inserted his clawed hand inside his enemy's chest.

The griffin dropped dead.

"That's our target, Nephilim."

Bellum nodded as he watched the bat rip its enemy to shreds as it landed on the roof facing him.

"Bellum…" The Bat Said.

"Lovely to see you too, Onyc. It's been a long time."

Onyc was aware that the Nephilim didn't come just by coincidence. He had been hiding in this cathedral for the last ten thousand years as the Council asked in order to protect what they gave him. The Bat King was ready for a battle, yet he was curious as to what brought one of the Four to his domain.

"I know you're here because you need something…I know…" Onyc tried to reason with his visitor.

"I just wanted to send the Council's regards for you, Bat, and tell you how good of a job you're doing protecting the power they gave you."

"Cut the bullshit, Horseman! What is it you want?"

"Heaven and Hell have been engaged in an open war and the one who lit the fire under this conflict is still missing. I want to find him."

"War you say? I've lived here for thousands of years with minimal to no visitors, Bellum. Do you really expect me to know what you're talking about?"

"Whether you know or not, Onyc, I am here for information! I need to know what you know."

"What I know is far less than what you have in your arsenal of knowledge, Nephilim."

"*Fine*! I'll cut the crap and small talk! I want your heart, Bat! I'm not here to play games! Ursus said…"

"*Ursus*? You work for him now? Do you remember what he did thousands of years ago? He sinned, and you know it, Bellum, and now you want to help him?"

"It's the only way! The Council recommended seeking the help of Vulgar who, in turn, said that to protect everyone Ursus must be revived. The real Ursus! Only then I can reach Shaman and find out the truth!"

Onyc stood there, confused. What truth was the Nephilim talking about? What was happening in the world now? The Bat King had been residing in this cathedral for thousands upon thousands of years, ever since Ursus committed the first sin. He then remembered something the Council told him along with his brothers, the other chosen ones, about this moment.

"The day will come when one of the Four will ride against our will and seek vengeance. When that day comes, you will fight for honor and glory as you battle to slay the enemy and protect the Balance. Are you ready to fight for peace?" the Council asked.

"Yes my Lord," the chosen ones replied in unison.

"Then, go! Each of you will choose a place for him to live, but be warned… Wherever you choose to reside will be your house until the day of reckoning comes."

"We understand." Distepia replied, "For the Balance! For the peace!"

Onyc seemed in a daze, some sort of daydream. "What truth are you talking about, Nephilim?"

"All those years trapped here have made you lose focus of what is real, Onyc. Creation is in grave peril. Someone or some…thing has destroyed the seals that protected the peace we worked so hard to protect. I heard a call and was summoned to find an all-out war between Anxo's and Draxus's armies."

"How can this be, Horseman? The last seal hasn't been broken yet! I see why the Council sent you. In the middle of the conflict, you stood there alone facing both armies. You are accused of starting this."

"I am innocent, Onyc! Know your place, Bat! Know who you're talking to!"

"Oh, I do know, Nephilim, do you? I'm in the presence of a guilty Nephilim who tried to play hero and protect something that never existed. Did you think the peace will be eternal? As long as Heaven and Hell have their respective leaders, peace will never be fulfilled!"

"Both kingdoms always had rulers. What do you mean?"

"You are so delusional! Our master wants to crush Heaven and claim it as his own! That's how we will achieve a long-lasting peace! Take one piece of the puzzle away and replace it with the piece you want."

"Dragan's disciple you are, then!" Bellum grabbed his sword with both hands. "There is no going back for you, Bat King! You will fall by my blade."

"If that's what makes you sleep at nights, Horseman! You are allowed to wish and dream, yet we both know the outcome of this battle!"

"The only thing I believe in is my blade, Bat, and it has never failed me before!"

Onyc's face fell faster than a corpse in cement boots. In that instant his skin became red, his mouth hung down and his eyes were as wide as they could stretch. There wasn't even a point in searching in attempting to gain the Horseman as an ally. He had nothing but empty words. He glanced nervously at his visitor. If he didn't know that his life was more valuable than his death, he would've already been dead. Then, all bets were off.

"Horseman…I cannot imagine all the horror that's happening out there in this world, but I cannot, on the other hand, help revive Ursus's full power. You know as well as I do that, he will betray you and take a go at ultimate power, again I might add."

"Do not play the sympathy card with me, Bat. Beings like you have nothing but hatred and greed dwelling inside them." The Nephilim held his blade.

“We can do this the easy way or my way. Your choice, fiend.”

“Ursus will never get his powers back!” Onyc snapped an attacking stance. “Over my dead rotten corpse!”

“I really was hoping you would say that!”

There was stillness on both sides, as both Bat and Nephilim stood facing each other. No attacks or even attempts; they were just studying battle scenarios in their minds. If hatred was visible, the air would have been as hard as ice. Suddenly movement. Much force in every blow.

Bellum rained blows onto Onyc as if he meant to smash him into the very earth and the bat king did the same. Each didn't just want the other dead, they wanted him smashed, obliterated, nothing left to bury. When it came to attacking, no one ever played by "the rules." They aimed to get back to their lives, to their routine. In a way they saw it as defense, just taking it to each other when they weren't expecting it. As the enemies were battling it out, Nephilim and Bat King, Bellum noticed something strange in the form of a glowing splinter stuck in the Bat’s tail.

“What’s that, Nephilim?”

“This is not the time to distract me, watcher! Ursus has to have the hearts.”

"Nephilim...Do not disregard what you are seeing here. If that's what I think it is then you, we, are one step closer to finishing the job."

"Right, we have to find out what that thing is before it's too late."

"How are you planning on getting that high? You are a mere Nephilim with no flying abilities."

"I have my ways, watcher. Stop distracting me until I figure this out."

The youngest of the Four was quick to draw the edged cutlass he wielded and whipped around to clash steel. He held the blade, now in the shape of a chain, twirled it, and took a massive throw at the bat king. The chain hit! The bat king was surprised to see this type of attack from this particular nephilim. The chain was Ila's specialty. How could he use that technique?

"You cannot win this!" Onyc throatily crooned.

"You can bet that I will, Onyc. You are no match for one of the Four, even if you do possess the heart of a Chosen!"

"This heart is fueled by my master! The Council lost control over it years ago. Dragan took it over and showed me real power, power far more satisfying than what that mere Council presented to me! I will use it to kill you!"

"Brag while you can!" Bellum reached the bat's wing where the chain hit. "My face will be the last you see before your soul becomes history!"

Curiosity filled the Nephilim's mind and body as he wondered what that thing was sticking out of the Bat's tail. The Bat King was hesitant to use the fire breath he acquired from his master because his enemy was on his body and he didn't want to inflict self-damage. Bellum was the one with the upper hand as he scaled the beast's body, making way to whatever was at the tip of the tail. The Bat King couldn't comprehend what the Nephilim was up to, so he continued trying several attacks, but in vain. Bellum scaled the whole perimeter of his enemy's body and was able to reach the strange object. As he laid his hand on it, the piece glowed gold and attached itself to *Comedentis.*

"Horseman," the blade whispered, "What is this strange object attached to me?"

Bellum had no answer for his comrade. *Comedentis* had been his companion for over ten thousand years, and that moment was the first time he had no answer. "I don't know what that is, but whatever it may be how is it affecting you, friend?"

"Power…more power. It feels heavenly. All this power."

"So, this is helping you. I'm glad you feel comfortable as you hold it. When this is over, we will find out what that thing is and to get it detached from you, friend."

"Let's finish this, friend. We have more pressing matters to attend to. Dragan must go down, and his reign must be destroyed!"

Let's end this, comrade. It's all you now! Lend me your power and strength!"

Bellum had a job to do and he was not going to let anyone or anything stand in his way. He swiftly swung his blade and cut the beast from head to belly, then stood there watching as the Bat King smashed the ground with an impact of an earthquake, an earthquake that shattered the cathedral's roof on impact. The Horseman fell from the roof until he hit the ground.

As he stood and looked around, he found himself back at the entrance of the location. The watcher sighed. He knew going back up was a pain when the stairs are nonexistent anymore, yet what he didn't bargain for was that the Bat King slammed the ground right next to them. As the smoke from the wreckage faded, Bellum was able to spot the area where the Bat King fell.

"Well done, Horseman. Now, tear his heart out and let me hear Onyc scream!"

"Nephilim, please don't take my heart! Ursus must never gain back his powers. I can grant you any wish you desire if you have mercy to spare my life!"

"Can you restore the Balance? Can you bring Mankind back? Can you tell me who Dragan is and what he's up to?"

"Balance? You think it still exists? You are more of an idiot than we ever thought, Bellum!"

"Balance shall be restored, Bat, and you along with everyone you serve will perish!"

"Horseman! The Balance is imaginary. The Council hides behind the Balance they created in order to keep control over a realm that is not theirs to begin with!"

"The Council brought peace to this realm eons ago! Their job is to keep this peace and keep all the kingdoms safe!" Onyc laughed as Bellum sliced his chest and reached for his heart. The lights danced across the dark sky as the Nephilim grabbed the Bat King's beating heart, each color slowly fading into another. His body was tired from the intense battle he had to go through, but he couldn't care less. The lights were beautiful, swaying and changing and illuminating the world.

They could make any being's heart melt. Their glow, their shine, everything about them was beautiful. At that same moment, the sky turned to blood red as Ursus appeared standing next to the Bat King's fading corpse.

"Ursus! How did you get here?"

"You are lost to our race's mighty powers, Horseman. We have the ability to track down other essences that belong to our race. Since the power confined in this heart is mine, I am able to track its whereabouts and teleport to it. Hand me the heart of the first Chosen as you move one step closer to your goal!"

"The Bat said things about you! He said you are planning to overthrow the Council and claim this realm as your own."

"Is that so? And do you believe the gossip you got? Aren't you the one searching for Dragan? If he reigns supreme as we speak, that means that he has power like no other being."

"What are you hinting, fiend?"

"You see, Nephilim. If I had that kind of power, I wouldn't be here asking you to slay the Chosen and returning the hearts to me. Would I?"

"True, but what if this was a set up to gain even more power. Have you forgotten about your action then thousand years ago, or should I remind you?"

"I recall, Nephilim, no need to bring up mistakes I regret. Do you want to get to Dragan and redeem yourself?"

"This is my only purpose ever since the Council sent me back!"

"Then hand over the heart and let me help you." Bellum threw the heart in front of Ursus and watched in disgust as the ancient one fed on it.

"Well done, Bellum. Now, you must find the second of the Chosen. He is Talpa, the Mole. You will find him in his cave under the Deserted Ashland. Bring me his heart and you shall be rewarded."

"Any allies in that area?"

"Raven will be of great help to you along this quest. To defeat the Mole, you have to use unique tactics and think outside the box, Nephilim. No mortal or immortal weapon can damage him for his body is protected by a layer of crystallized armor."

"Very well, fiend. I will find my way around that Chosen and bring you what you want. But remember this. If you ever think about double crossing one of the Four your punishment will be far more severe than just confinement. Are we clear on that?"

"I never forget what did this to me and who did it. I know where my loyalty lays, Horseman. I hope you know where yours lies."

"You speak of loyalty as if you know what it is, ancient one. Don't forget who slaughtered his mother for no reason. Keep that in mind when you feel enough rage to try and kill me."

"I never forget a face or a memory, Nephilim, specially a memory like that one!"

"I will be on my way, then." Bellum turned his back to his "ally" and headed to the caves.

Chapter VI
Unplanned Rescue

Bellum was content with his victory over the Bat King, yet he had a long way to go. As Ursus teleported back to his tower, the Nephilim stood there, confused. How would he find Raven again? *She definitely left the battlefield and headed back to the forest* he thought to himself, but where was the forest located? It wasn't like he knew how he got there in the first place; he just teleported there from Ursus' tower. Thoughts ran through his head as he tried to figure out what to do next and where to go.

Raven was the only being that knew where to go. He needed someone to guide him in the right direction so he could at least start walking. As he looked around searching for an exit, Bellum saw, with the corner of his eye, a familiar face; it was Vulgar.

"How did you get here, Demon?"

"Ursus is not the only one who has the power to teleport, Nephilim. I am a being of many…talents."

"The only talent you have, Demon, is leeching your only source of life off beings that are able to hunt souls for your pleasure!"

"The Council left me with nothing after mercilessly annihilating my family! The only source of food was souls. I had to change, to become something I never wanted to be, a beggar."

"Haven't you always been a beggar, demon? Even before all of this, all the killing and destruction, you were a beggar merchant, Demon."

"That was business, Horseman! You can't expect a mere merchant to be living off some scraps in a world where it's kill or be killed!"

"Even so, Vulgar."

"I had no choice!"

"You had a choice when you killed your son! You had a choice when the Council offered help! And you certainly had a choice when the Four came for you!"

"What would they—"

"They could've helped you! You knew that killing family was a sin! You had a front row seat when you watched Ursus receive his punishment! The Council was so lenient to do what they did to you! You should be in cuffs, or worse, dead! Your current status is on your hands! You did this to yourself!"

"This is no time to dwell on the past, on what could've been, Horseman. I did this to myself and I live in remorse every passing moment. What is it that you require of me, Nephilim?"

"I need a path back to the forest where Raven resides."

"Ah, yes. The Demented Forest is what you seek, Horseman. This information isn't cheap."

"How do I get there, Demon? I need to find Raven again."

"The Demented Raven, hmmm…"

"Demented?"

"You have an idea of her past, don't you, Horseman? There were stories about a female being that could slaughter armies with a single blow at will."

"I've seen it for myself. Back when we fought the Angels. She killed everyone with one attack, one spell."

"That's why heaven and hell call her the Demented Raven. No one in the right mind would ever dare to cross her. Though she looks like a little child, she has potential."

"Where is she now?"

"Unfortunately, Nephilim, I can't track her. She is one of the few who could stay under the radar for as long as she wanted. The forest isn't a place you can find by just looking. It's a place in your mind, in your thoughts. The only way in and out is through Raven herself. All I can tell you is that you are on the right path. Head west from here and seek the marks of the Demented one, only then you may be able to find her."

How could I leave my only ally in all of this chaos all alone in a forest with soldiers around her? How could I be so stupid? He thought as he made his way west, just like the merchant advised him. Bellum was in total disbelief. He felt so cold as if the sun disappeared and a freezing wind took over. It occurred to him that it must be a nightmare. As he walked along the path his vision diminished. He had no rest after his battle with the bat king, and with no time at all he dropped unconscious.

When Bellum came back to his senses and woke up, he found himself lying next to a small river. He lay the exact same place he was the day he met Raven. He noticed something different about the forest; it wasn't as pretty as I used to be. The grass changed color, and the trees bent to the side while some were destroyed. Blood scattered everywhere gave the green grass a new intense red dye.

It was a massacre.

As he walked amidst the destruction in front of him, his blade's voice echoed in his mind, "Do you see what I see, Nephilim?"

"I see it, comrade."

"This was no ordinary battle. The being that did this was out of his mind."

"I can only think of one person with so much power. Ra—"

"Raven! Vulgar was right, she is demented! How can one being cause so much destruction?"

"Self-defense, I presume."

"What makes you come to this conclusion, Horseman?"

"Look around you, watcher. How many corpses can you see? This forest is Raven's sanctuary. She won't cause so much destruction without a good reason. She must've been attacked. That was self-defense."

"Who would think about attacking this place? The better question is how did they get here?"

"Examine the corpses." The Nephilim approached one of the dead bodies. "The hearts are cleaved from the bodies. The bodies are dry, no blood remains in the veins of the dead, which allows me to deduce that this battle happened a while ago, maybe when we were on our way to the Cathedral. The face is pale. This must have been torture."

As he continued examining the bodies around him, Bellum found that one clue he was waiting for, a dead body of an Angel with a broken wing. The body was so bloody as if it were newly killed. One of the wings was folded, broken in half, while the other was detached. On that body, was a message written in blood.

The Message Said:

You took something valuable and close to my heart! I cannot keep quiet and let it slide. I will take everything from you, Nephilim bastard. If you want to see your little friend alive again, you will follow my every command and do as I say!

I have my eyes on you, Bellum. If you try and disobey me, she dies. If you try to find other allies, she dies. And if you ever ask the help of Anxo I will cut her limbs and send them one by one. If you want to get your friend back, I dare you to invade the Holy City and save her. The soul of my griffin shall be avenged!' ~ Alma "Raven is just a child and she has nothing to do with what I am after. Why would Alma attempt to hurt Raven? I should've taken her with me to Onyc's cathedral! I should've protected her!"

"This isn't on you, Horseman." The watcher said, "Even if you took her with you, what guarantees did you have that she wouldn't get hurt during the fight? Or worse, die?"

"There was none! Yet it was better than having her kidnapped by an Angel and taken to the Holy City!"

"Horseman! We have to get her back! As much as I hate to admit this, Raven helped you on the journey for the first Chosen."

"She did. She is my only ally in the middle of all this chaos. Alma will pay with her life! She will learn the hard way not to cross one of the Four!" Bellum headed toward the Holy City.

His heart filled with anger, as he kept thinking about the real motives behind taking Raven into the Holy City. Was it a trap? To have one of the Four storm the city when it posed no threat against Creation? Make the Four look as the ones who want to destroy Creation? Not to mention that Bellum and his brethren were banned from the Holy City after *Mors* last attacked it few centuries ago and stole the pendant of souls, so going there to find Raven was a suicide mission. The story between the Four and the Holy City went back thousands of years ago.

The time had come when the Four would last cleanse Creation, but before that could be done, they needed to secure the forbidden weapons. The weapons were forged by the Anaiim race and used mainly by the Council's champions, when needed, to help the process of cleansing. Mors, being the eldest of the Four, was the only one capable of locating the weapons.

"Brother, what is the next step for us?"

"Us? There is no us in this journey. Bellum, as the eldest, I compel you not to risk your lives for me. I will go at this alone." Mors replied.

"Are you insane? You are not going alone. We had your back for years, and we are not about to sit here and watch you walk to your demise!"

"Ila's right, our mission is to keep Creation safe and the peace between Angels and Demons permanent. Why do you forbid us from doing our duty?" Discordia asked.

"If you only knew where my duty takes me you would shake in terror of merely the name." Mors turned his back.

"Mors, you cannot leave us out of this! Tell us what's the mission, and where."

"Do you recall, brethren, a race called the Anaiim? They were forgers responsible for making weapons for the Council's champions. They were formidable weapons that contained great power passed down from the Council itself; however, used in the wrong way, they have the ability to destroy realms and bring civilizations to the ground."

"How is that even possible? How come we never heard of these weapons?"

"The Anaiim were famous for using the bones of their fallen enemies to forge weapons. They refined those bones, adding some of their own souls, to fabricate weapons. They were so powerful that the Council forbids using them unless the situation demands it, a last resort. As the eldest, I was the only one entrusted with the information about these weapons and the

only one responsible for retrieving them and make sure they get destroyed."

"Brother, you are not alone. Not in this mission or any other. We have your back." Ila put her hand on his shoulder.

"I have made up my mind, Brothers. I go alone." He gave Bellum, what looked like a crystal sphere, "Take this. It will show you my location and will reveal whatever events occur on my mission."

"Where does this mission take you, Brother?"

"The Holy City, Discordia."

"The Hol—"

"What in the Council's name! Are you insane? Storming that place alone is a suicide mission!" Ila said.

"Brother! Don't do this. Let us help you," Discordia said.

"This burden is mine and mine alone." Mors held his scythe, "Potentia Concilii audite vocem meam, accipe a me, ut ubi malum est. Tolle mihi civitatem Sanctam."

With those few words, Mors left the area leaving his brethren in total disbelief as he teleported to his destination. The city was standing tall on a green hill at the edge of Eden, buildings made of pure gold surrounded by the highest of walls. Mors wasn't intimidated by the sight of the city as he stood facing the entrance, scythe in hand.

"Potentia antiquis locus vetita arma, conservare eos, et perdere omnia," *he said, turning into his reaper form. The spell had the city fall to ground. The Holy City was destroyed! Nothing remained of the outer shell of the city as the buildings fell one by one leaving nothing but rubble in their place.*

"Why do you attack Heaven, Pale Rider?"

"Anxo…I wish I can say it's a pleasure to meet you, but this isn't the time for formalities."

"How dare you attack the Holy City!? This is a holy site and no place for a Nephilim!"

"Hand over the forbidden weapons hidden in this city or face the wrath of the Council!"

"The. Forbidden. Weapons. How do you even know they are here?"

"You forget your place in Creation, Archangel. I am older than even you. I supervised the creation of these abominations which allowed me to insert soul magic into each one. That magic is my source of information. Hand them over, unless you want to see everything your ancestors worked for get pummeled?"

Anxo looked around scanning the damage done by Mors's spell. Nothing remained form the once great city.

"Very well, rider, take them! But you have to promise that none of you shall ever return to the Holy City! Not now, not ever!"

"My brothers are watching my every move through a crystal sphere I left behind. I'm sure they will abide by this deal as well. From this day forth, the Four shall be banned from

stepping inside the city of Angels!" Mors recovered the weapons and teleported out.

With that memory in mind, Bellum knew he had no choice but to head to the city to confront Alma and save Raven. The city was magnificent, as sight for sore eyes especially after seeing all the destruction at the cathedral. Buildings towered the land in a valley between two snowy mountains. Back to its former glory, the city shone in the light of the mid-day sun. It looked even better than he remembered seeing through the crystal sphere.

"I can't just simply walk inside the city. This is the home for heaven's army, to Anxo and Alma."

"Horseman. You have to find your way around the city without being detected. We cannot waste time engaging in unnecessary fights. It's important that we get in and get out as fast we could."

"Every Angel wants me dead, even their leader and general. Damn you, Mors! Damn you for destroying this city!"

"Ah, yes, the legend of Mors the destroyer of the Holy City. It's because of him that you can't knock on the door and step in."

"There must be an entrance somewhere far from the guards, I cannot be seen or interrupted. Raven is priority."

"The sewers," the watcher looked towards a crack in the lower wall that surrounded the city, "There!"

The Nephilim made his way through the opening into the sewers where no one resided. The smell was so common with the stench of dirty water and dead rats. Walking around the sewers searching for a way out, Bellum noticed another crack in the wall with light escaping his location. He was out of the sewers in the middle of a small alleyway between the houses.

As he walked the streets of the city, the Nephilim couldn't find any living soul; maybe all were hiding in fear from his presence. It seemed like he would never find a single clue leading to Alma's whereabouts; that was until he heard a female's voice, "No one will come to help you, little girl!"

"Arrgh ye sure aboot that, lady?"

That's Raven's voice, Bellum thought. *No one else has that accent and that fierce tone while talking. She must be saved. This is my chance to interfere and get her out of here.*

"Alma!" Bellum barged through the door, "You are not going to get away with this! How dare you kidnap her!? She's just a child!"

"Who ye calli—" Raven tried to explain when Alma interrupted her.

"You took away my best friend, Horseman!"

"I killed no one! Your Griffin was the one who killed itself. It rushed into battle to protect me against the bat king!"

"D—E—F – E – N – D you? Why would he defend the likes of you when the only thing you did is injure me and kidnap him?"

"He did his job! Unlike you he protected those who needed help. You pretend to be the saviors of Creation, but all you do is accuse the innocent!"

"We defend the weak! We are the protect—"

"You are nothing, Alma! Protectors don't kidnap! Saviors don't falsely accuse the innocent of any sin! They see everyone as equal! You save Raven the same way you save me or any other being in this realm! I am not going to fight you! We are on the same side!"

"Fight or not it's your choice, Horseman!" Alma held her blade. "Killing you will be easier than I thought!"

Their swords gleamed in the moonlight. Bellum knew that only one would walk away from this. His opponent's sword was stained with blood from cutting his body. He shuffled to the side and waited an attack as his opponent charged with a mighty cry.

Alma thrust her sword forward, only to be met by Bellum's. Both swords met in the air with a resounding clang. The general Angel was a master swordsman, but so was he. What seemed to be an endless battle was suddenly halted by a powerful presence over the battle area.

"Alma!" the voice shook the sky above the arena, "How dare you sin?"

"A.....A.....Anxo? M...M....My lord I have done nothing of that sort!"

"Silence! You are not to talk unless I address you! As for you, Nephilim, you have been warned not to enter the Holy City under death threats. Leave before the death sentence is executed!"

"I just came here for my friend! Your disciple was the one who kidnapped her and lead me here knowing that my brethren and I are banned from the walls of this city!"

"Alma! I've taught you better than this! You can't go around kidnapping people!"

"He took my Griffin! He killed it! He—"

"Silence! If the Griffin sensed danger, he would've tried to dismount the Nephilim! You know that better than anyone, Alma! You raised thousands in your life!"

"But—"

"But nothing! I will deal with you later!" he looked at the Horseman, "Nephilim. Take your friend and leave the city. No one wants another incident inside these walls. Take her and leave! Head my words, Nephilim, the next time we meet you won't be so lucky."

"So be it, Angel. So be it." Bellum grabbed Raven's arm and yanked her toward him as he made his way to the field outside the city back to the Demented Forest.

"Thank ye, Nephilim." Raven grinned.

"I didn't save you because I liked you, kid. I saved you because you are of use to me still. When this is over, I could care less where you go and what you do."

"But, still, ye saved my life." The smirk on Raven's face grew more visible.

"What are you smiling about, kid? We have more work to do!"

"Ye searching for the second Chosen, I reckon." Raven went to her library. She began searching the ancient scribes like a mad woman on a mission.

"Indeed, kid. I search the location of Talpa, the Demon Mole."

"Aye. He lives in the caves under the desert, Horseman." Raven took out a scroll from the library.

"So, I've been informed, kid. Ursus has filled me in on the Demon, everything except how to defeat it."

"Here it is." Raven ignored the Nephilim's last comment, "This will help ye on yer journey. *Magicae telum meam audiunt, vocant. Ego praecipio tibi accipere forma dominum tuum desiderium. Da vires ad auxilium eum in sua investigatione pro redemptione."*

The words that came out of the Maker's mouth was an ancient incantation only studied by her kind, passed from generation to generation every hundred years. Bellum stood there with no idea what Raven was doing. Suddenly, his blade began to glow.

"The power of your blade is limited by your own imagination, Nephilim. The spell I placed on your companion allows it to change form to your desire. Use it wisely, Horseman. You seek the second Chosen. Head toward the caves beneath the Desert. That's where you will find it. Be careful how you use your companion, Horseman."

Chapter VII
The Caves

The first heart was delivered. The Nephilim's next step was finding the second Chosen and get its heart. As he walked to the cave's entrance, he was interrupted by his companion's voice.

"What did she mean when she said *use* it wisely?" *Comedentis* asked, "What am I some kind of tool now?"

"Do not mind her words, comrade. You are my companion. Together, we will find redemption. Don't mind some stupid comments from beings who don't know what you truly are."

"She insulted me! *Me*! The most powerful holy weapon of all! How dare she?"

"Calm down, friend, she doesn't really know how to express herself very well. Don't think of it as an insult. See it more as like acknowledging that you have abilities."

With those words, the Nephilim soothed the blade's thoughts. *Comedentis* was like no other comrade. It was the only blade that could ever steal the life essence of its victims. With this power its wielder had the ability to practically live forever. As the Horseman walked, he could sense the presence of a powerful being; he couldn't see it, but he could feel its spiritual energy around the area.

"Do you feel that, Horseman?" the watcher whispered.

"This is not good. I sense something more powerful than even Ursus."

"Could it be the Chosen we are after?"

"*We*? *We* are not after shit! I am after it. I will kill it. And I will redeem myself, for my brethren and for myself!"

"Yes…Yes…You Nephilim, all you."

"Watch your tongue, watcher!"

"I apologize, Horseman."

"You better be sorry! You are just a filthy burden that the Council put on my shoulders! Never think for one moment that your life means anything to me!"

"Yes. I'm but a mere watcher. My life isn't worth anything."

"I'm glad you know your place in this realm! Now, keep quiet!"

Before the watcher could even finish uttering his words, they found themselves standing at a huge entrance made of pure gold with a hint of diamonds. It was glorious! Both Nephilim and watcher were astonished at this marvel.

This is it. This is what I'm looking for and here is where I will find the second Chosen. Your heart is mine, Mole. Be prepared for the fight of your life, he thought.

As the door opened in front of them, they could see the outline of a wonder. Crystals everywhere; it was like the whole cave was carved into a large crystal. Bellum made his way through the cave still taken by its beauty. He had never seen such a creation.

"Focus, Nephilim," the watcher interrupted.

"Watcher! I know why I'm here. Shut it, unless you prefer I shut it for you!"

"Remember where your loyalty resides, Horseman. You serve the Council. And I am but a mere puppet in their hands. My life is worth nothing to them or to you."

"Does it matter to you?"

It was silence from the not so trusty companion. Bellum only trusted his blade and his brethren, no one else. The path they followed lead to a vast spacious room also decorated with crystals, centering it was a giant throne made of pure gold.

"This is it…" the watcher murmured, "This is the throne room!"

"It is, indeed. But where is the second Chosen?"

The ground shook, and the crystals rattled all throughout the forbidden cave. Then, a huge monster appeared. It had spider legs with huge mandible claws that could snap any being into two pieces easily. The Mole was huge, a giant with a crystal for a stomach.

"Nephilim…You have come for me as expected." The Mole said.

"And you're surprised. Why?"

"Since the news of my brethren Onyc's, death I figured I will be next. However, Horseman, I am not as an easy prey as my brother."

"You dare threaten one of the Four!? We shall see how you deal with a foe like me!"

"You don't know who you're talking to, boy! I am Talpa the King Mole, ruler of this realm's underground!"

"You think that'll impress me? A king who never leaves his kingdom. Who doesn't know what the outside world has to offer! Do you even think that you're worthy of calling yourself a king? If you're a king where are all your subjects? A ruler has to have subordinates, or have they taken a trip down belly-lane!?"

"Mock all you want, Horseman! With their souls sacrificed I gain more strength! More than you could ever imagine!"

"Strength isn't everything, Talpa! Heart and will are what count! And in this fight you seem to have none!"

"There's another way, boy. You can join us...We can grant you whatever your heart, if you had one, wants. Our master is very fond of you, Bellum, and he wants to have you on his team."

"Ally with Dragan!? Do you think I am that stupid? He was the reason I am accused of being a traitor! He is the reason I was imprisoned by the Council! I will never join evil! He will die and so will you!"

"Boy, I'll warn you, I'll not go easy on you just because you're one of the Four!"

"I wouldn't want it any other way!" Bellum held his blade over his shoulder with one hand. The fight broke out loose on the battlefield that consisted of a crystallized floor in a vast empty room. Swing after swing from the Nephilim's blade didn't hit the mark. On the other hand, the Mole landed his shots injuring his opponent.

Bellum was knocked down. *I cannot lose this! I have to redeem myself and clear the name of the Four. It's all on me now!* Thoughts tortured the Nephilim's mind as a memory fluctuated inside his brain about the time he was with Raven sitting on the wooden bench. He could recall some words of incantation Raven spoke as she assured him that he was going to be okay.

"The power of your blade is limited by your own imagination, Nephilim." Raven explained, "The spell I placed on your companion allows it to change form to your desire. Use it wisely."

Bellum's ears rang heavily as he started recalling the spell that Raven had put on his blade. "*Magicae telum meam audiunt, vocant. Ego praecipio tibi accipere forma dominum tuum desiderium. Da vires ad auxilium eum in sua investigatione pro redemption,*" he said.

Without any warning, *Comedentis* started to glow and a supernova heat emerged to burn the blade's enemy. No one knew what was actually happening, yet Bellum went with it.

"This burns!" the Mole screamed as his claws lit up with fire.

"I warned you fighting one of the Four had its consequences," Bellum replied.

"You will never win you idiot swine! You will never win! Our master will have this world and whatever other worlds exist! We are power! We are inevitable!"

The words could not get out of the monster's mouth because of all the pain it was in from burning claws. However, the Nephilim couldn't see it suffer any longer, and with the help of his upgraded blade, he cut off both large claws. Even without the claws, Bellum couldn't find the location of the second heart.

Where can it be? It is not like other creatures where the heart is high in the upper body. Wait… The Horseman had an eye opener. *Why is the monster's lower body covered with crystal? Is the heart in there? How can I get that heart? I'm sure that's no ordinary crystal.* With that thought, *Comedentis* transformed into the form of a gauntlet.

"Wait…What happened?" the blade questioned.

"That's what the Maker meant when she said, "Use it wisely." Don't you think, comrade?" Bellum replied.

"It is what it is, my friend."

With that being said, Bellum smashed the crystal that covered the Mole's lower body. As it shattered to millions of tiny pieces, the monster dropped to the ground.

"No… please." The Mole pleaded, "Please, do not take the heart. I can grant you your deepest desires."

"That is what your brother Onyc said as well as he was lying on the ground in a pool of his own stinky blood. So I ask of you what he could not do. Can you restore the Balance?"

"Balance? There is no Balance to talk about! It never existed! You have been fighting for some ghost the Council convinced you it existed! You are fighting for nothing! We are inevitable!"

"When you meet your brethren, Taalpa, send him my regards." Bellum said as his blade was a sword again, "Tell him how you felt when my blade touched your skin. Pain changes a being, 'specially a being with no soul."

Those were the Nephilim's final words as he grabbed the second heart and ripped it form the crystallized body that once nested it. The Mole was gone, back down to the depths of Creation where he was made. With that quest complete, Ursus appeared once again in the center of the room.

"Well done, Horseman." Ursus was pleased at what he saw.

"Why are you so surprised? I am one of the Four. Here is the second heart you requested."

As Ursus devoured the heart, a black smoke emerged from his body while all his damaged limbs and features were restored to their original self.

"My body has been restored. Thank you, Horseman." He admired his newly found physical condition.

"No time for appreciation and gratitude, fiend. We have to move and find the third heart. Where can I find it?"

"Straight to business. The third Chosen is called Deathworm. She roams the desert directly above this cave. As her name suggests, she is a giant worm-like creature with no soul, lives underground. She goes to the surface only to feed on her victims! She feeds on whatever she finds; humans, Goblins, anything!"

"I'm sure the desert is a dangerous place from what I know, Ursus. Any other creatures I should be aware of going to that area?"

"Yes, Horseman! A clan of Goblins has seized the desert and now they live there! They were able to wipe every other being in the premises and take over the whole deserted area."

"If Deathworm possesses so much strength and power and is able to feed on almost everything, how are the Goblins able to escape it?"

Ursus didn't look surprised as the Nephilim asked that question, "The Goblin chief possesses a weapon called the Chronotek. Whoever has this weapon in his arsenal is able to slow down time and even pause it at will. With the Chronotek, the Goblins can travel safely across the desert. They can hide from the worm's killing instincts."

"The million souls question remains, fiend, how can I defeat the Deathworm?"

"Ah…That is the right question to ask, Bellum. The beast has four sets of teeth inside its giant mouth. The glands that fill the gaps between the teeth are filled with flammable liquids. Ignite them and the Worm Queen is dead."

"Any advice about how to ignite it?"

"The glands are protected by metal armor. The task will not be easy, Horseman, yet you have proved yourself very resourceful." Ursus vanished out of sight.

Bellum sat on the throne that centered the battlefield when the watcher appeared next to him, "Why are you so hesitant, Nephilim?" he asked.

"It's not hesitation…I am thinking about a way to obtain the third heart since Ursus was no help at all."

"We have no time to sit and think. We need to get going."

"I have to get moving, watcher. You are correct, for once. I will think of a plan on my way to face the worm queen. Let's go!"

"You have proved yourself very resourceful, Horseman. With all the abilities you acquired along the way, I'm sure the worm queen will pose no threat to you."

"Don't underestimate the power of a Chosen one, puny watcher! You had front row seats for the previous battles, and you saw what they're capable of!"

"True—"

"Then, keep quiet and let me think about the information Ursus granted me! The third Chosen will not be as easy as we thought!"

Silence dominated the air as the nephilim and his comrades stepped outside the cave's exit heading towards the desert above, Deathworm's domain.

Chapter VIII
The Deathworm's Domain

With the second Chosen eliminated, Bellum began to focus on the new task ahead, the Deathworm. Thoughts circled his head about that creature. *Why was this creature created? The Council could have chosen any other being to grant such power to, why her?* The Nephilim came up empty on answers and remained confused. That was until the watcher appeared.

"It's time for the third heart, Horseman. You can't reach your final destination without it."

"Tell me something I do not know, filth! You dare question my capability to handle myself? Tell me what to do? Who do you think you are?" Bellum grabbed his companion by the throat.

"I am but a mere servant. I said it before and I will say it again, Nephilim, my life doesn't matter."

"Shut your hole! You are nothing, and you will always be nothing! Now moving on to more....pressing matters."

Bellum glanced left and right in search of a way out of the caves. What he got instead surprised both him and the watcher. "Vulgar?" the Nephilim asked surprised to see the Demon.

"Seems we have a nag of always meeting, Horseman. How can I be of service to one of the Four?"

"What are you doing here, fiend? Last time we met; we were at the cathedral where I slayed the Bat King."

"I am here to help, Bellum. I hear you need a passageway out of the caves. I can grant you that, for a price, of course."

"What can you give me that I do not already possess? I can find my way out of the caves without your help, Demon!"

"Nephilim….I possess talents others…frown upon. They include the secret passageways of the ancient Demons, the magic scripts of the most powerful of Angels, and everything in between."

"If you have so much power and know so many secrets, why didn't you try to help when the world needed you? You have the secrets of the Angels as you said so why not use them to prevent the extinction of Man!?" Bellum mocked.

"I may have the secrets, Nephilim, but I am not in a position to use them. I am always being watched by the Council's henchmen. Every move I make, every step I take, and everything is being watched by them. The only thing they do not know is what I tell my customers."

"And, that is?"

"In this world demons created the Sakian Tunnels."

"The tunnels…?" the watcher meddled in the middle of the conversation.

"Yes, filth, the tunnels," the merchant continued, "They are the passageways that Demons created to transport themselves from one location to another without being detected."

"So that's how you got to the Cathedral by the time Onyc was dead," Bellum concluded.

"Yes, Horseman. That was the way," the demon merchant continued, "Since you figured it out, Nephilim; I will award you a precious gift."

The Nephilim was so conflicted with himself. Was he to trust a demon when their race started this whole conflict? Would he be willing to risk his reputation and work with one? His heartbeats raced through the sky; they were more intense than the battle he had with the Mole.

"*Hoc ego det vobis donum cuniculis. Anima vestra, ut transeat illuc, ut tibi placuerit, et aliqua ratio appetit.* Horseman! I am your ally. The reward is access to the tunnels. You can now enter and exit them as you find suitable. Use them wisely, Bellum, and don't let any other being know of them." Vulgar's body faded away back to the tunnels which he emerged from.

Bellum stood there shocked after what Vulgar did. He thought all Demons were the same, evil and manipulating, but this mere merchant was different. Though he looked like a typical fiend, he was an ally, a second ally after Raven. The best way to thank the merchant was making good use of what he gave him.

Bellum made his way to the desert. The journey was short and straightforward. It was like being teleported in less than the time it took him to breathe. The desert was right there in front of them, so vast and desolate. Nothing to see except mountains of sand and nothing else. As the Nephilim walked through the area all he could see were bones and skeletons everywhere.

"This is a massacre," the watcher spoke, "How can one beast cause so much damage, so much death, so many casualties?"

"It…She has the power of the Council flowing in her veins. As the Chosen ones before her she is as strong as you might imagine."

"Strong or not, you have to finish the job, Horseman!"

"I know what I've got to do, filth! The job will be completed. You can bet your miserable life on that!"

Before his lips could finish the sentence, Bellum was greeted by a sight he never wanted to see, Goblins. An army of Goblins surrounded him each holding a primitive spear aimed at the Nephilim. As they circled him, the chief approached Bellum.

The chief wasn't familiar to the Nephilim, yet he couldn't help but feel he knew him from somewhere. *Wait…his horse! That's my horse! That is my steed. He has been with me for more than five thousand years. What the hell is this filth doing riding him?* Bellum thought.

"Horseman! What brings you here to these retched lands?" the general asked.

"Shut up, filth! How in Creation's name did you get your hands on that horse? That was my steed when I last rode to cleanse the land from evil alongside my brethren."

The Goblin general chuckled, "Your steed? You make jokes, Nephilim. Sathia is mine now. After you got yourself in the middle of this chaos the Council saw that I was fit for such a generous prize. You have lost your right to call him yours!"

Bellum wasn't pleased with the words that came out of the general. "Lost the right? I am one of the

Four; I lose no rights! You will not live long to enjoy your little 'prize,' general!"

"Don't be full of yourself, Nephilim. You are accused of rekindling the conflict between heaven and hell! Do you really think that you're still entitled to everything? You have nothing now!"

"I have my honor! I am innocent! The Council sent me back to this forsaken world to find the one truly responsible for this war!"

"Honor? You have nothing! Not even your brethren are here to save you!"

The Nephilim lunged at the Goblin general with an attempt at a surprise attack, and it worked. The chief fell off the horse and slammed his face in the desert sand. As he stood back up, he looked back at Bellum with flaming eyes, eyes you can only see rage and hatred in.

"You'll never have him back, Nephilim! He is mine and only mine! You'll have him over my dead body!"

Bellum smirked as he held his blade now in the form of two smaller daggers, "Let's end this quarrel, general." He started to pick up pace running at his foe. The Goblin chief had no chance of reaching his weapon; Bellum was too fast for him. With one swift slash the youngest of the Four beheaded his enemy.

As the general's head rolled on the hot sand, Sathia's eyes gazed at his master's face as it started to fade away. Suddenly, the steed's appearance began to shift as he turned into a shadow horse with smoke for hair, fire for eyes, and steel skulls as armor. He was enraged at his master's death that he charged the Horseman instinctively.

"Sathia!" Bellum yelled, "I will not fight you!"

Everything the Nephilim tried was unsuccessful. Hesitation and confusion took over his mind, as he had a flashback to the time when he first met Sathia.

Bellum, honey? Did you see what your father got you?" a tender voice asked.

"A present for me? What is it?" he said confused as he ran outside to meet his father.

"Son, I know you have been training hard to help us fight if the war ever broke loose again. And for you to be a Horseman you need a horse, so here you go." The man smiled gently as he brought out a small pony. The pony was beautiful, black as night with bright yellow eyes and light smoke as hair and tail.

"A shadow horse!?" little Bellum exclaimed. "For me? I don't know what to say. Thank you, Dad!"

"Now, Son," the male figure continued, "You know that to tame a shadow horse you should cast a spell."

The memory in Bellum's head became clear enough that he could remember every word of that incantation. However, he had no time to think or speak, as Sathia was running around trying to attack him several times. With the Nephilim's blade back to its original form, the big sword, he managed to swing and hit.

The shadow horse was stunned for a while. "*Umbra equus ortum et obedire. Criminis hostis, et tueri magister. Honora investigatione et adimplere desiderium tuum. Ardere Terram, ut gradum pedem in eius superficie. Videte verbum meum tenebitur ad dominum tuum,*" Bellum mumbled as the crest his forehead began to glow. At that instant, the stunned figure of the horse faded and a new body was summoned standing next to the Horseman, ready for battle.

"You are back, my friend." Bellum smiled as his new companion sniffled, "Now, let's get the Worm Queen."

Bellum rode his new steed and made his way to the find the Deathworm.

Hours later, the Horseman saw a fortress in the distance that had a tower holding the worm queen not allowing her to move.

"So that's what the Chronotek in capable of." The watcher gasped.

"I see..." the Nephilim replied as he stood astonished at what the Goblins had done.

As the Horseman approached the tower, the Goblins lined up protecting their domain from the visitor. The guard saw the general's horse in the distance heading towards the fortress, but the rider wasn't their leader. Before Bellum arrived at his destination, the Earth shook, and the sand began moving.

Suddenly, out of desperation, the Worm Queen made a final move by breaking the chains and setting itself free. Goblins ran around horrified of what this beast could do to them, while Bellum remained in place riding his horse. Deathworm was magnificent, long worm-like body with four sets of teeth sharp enough to eat through steel. On her mouth, there was a piece of metal protecting the flammable substance found in her glands, the glands that Ursus told him about, the only way to kill the beast.

The Worm Queen roamed the wasteland searching for preys to devour as Bellum followed the beast's path thinking of a way to expose whatever glands resided under the metal armor. He signaled Sathia to start his shadow run, that type of sprint allowed the horse to achieve higher running speed while consuming less stamina. That helped the rider reach the Worm Queen faster.

Bellum held his sword, now in the form of a gun, the same gun given to him by his brother Discordia, started shooting the Worm Queen as she devoured the whole Goblin army. All his efforts to draw the beast's attention went in vain; he had to think about a plan B. *What to do now?* He thought. *This is the third heart slipping away. I need to focus, to find another way.*

"Horseman," the watcher said as he barged the Nephilim's thought process, "What is the plan? We need that beast to focus on you."

"I know, watcher, I have a plan, but it involves getting destroyed by that thing."

"What do you mean destroyed?"

Bellum ignored the last question as he made his way closer to the Deathworm, holding his blade in his right hand now in the form of a pike; he scratches the surface skin of the beast. The worm queen pauses; turns around to face the Horseman.

The plan worked! Bellum thought as a giant smirk took over his face. *Now, let's end this. Comedentis,* now in the form of a gun yet again glowed with power, power it was drawing form the piece of the Blade of Eternals that was glued to it. With all the shots fired, and even with the power it had, *Comedentis* couldn't do damage to the worm queen. However, Bellum had other plans.

The Nephilim rode his horse to the front side of the monster and just poked it with his blade. The worm queen wasn't so fond of his actions, so she plunged down and swallowed Bellum. The insides of the beast were unlike any other beast he faced–no apparent organs and nothing to actually stab.

Bellum was struck of what he saw, but he wasn't out of it yet. As he searched for the third heart inside the Deathworm's body he was able to dodge many attacks from thorns and sharp teeth that made the body. What felt like hours of searching ended with the Nephilim spotting a glowing organ-like aperture stuck between the last row of teeth.

Before he could take a closer look, *Comedentis* glowed, and the shiny piece just flew from its position and glued itself to the blade as the weapon whispered, "*Excitare sensus et ecce invisibilium. Revelare occulta, et da potestatem sextus sensus. Videte verbum meum, et obedire!*"

The blade Bellum wielded had a new power now, sixth vision. Everything the Horseman saw was in heat vision now as his senses were connected to that of his companions.

"The heart!" the watcher pointed out as he turned Bellum's attention from his celebration.

"Silence yourself, watcher! With this new ability I will find it!"

And, there it was, the third heart. As soon as Bellum grabbed it, the Deathworm roared and screeched in pain, fell slamming the sand with such force that it destroyed everything around it for miles.

The Horseman took the heart out leaving the worm-like body to disappear with the flying sand.

"Impressive, Horseman!" a voice happily exclaimed from the distance.

"Ursus…How is it that you always know when to show up?"

"I can sense the power of my property. Hand it over and get to the last heart," Bellum threw the beating organ to the ground and had Ursus pick it up and devour it. The ancient one wasn't pleased with what the Nephilim did, but he wanted his powers back.

"You have done well. Now, for the last piece of the puzzle. Head to the edge of the desert. There you will find two pillars standing tall in a sea of corpses and blood; that's where you will find the entrance to the Capella."

"The Capella?" the watcher asked as his body shivered. Bellum could see that the watcher was uncomfortable with the words that came out of Ursus's mouth, but he gave it no attention as he wanted to wrap this conversation up as soon as he could.

"Very well, Ursus. Anything I should know about the forth Chosen?"

"She is the Spider Queen, Horseman, her name is Distepia. She dwells in the caves under the Capella and feeds of its victim's fear."

"Any allies?"

"Horseman, you are heading to the end of the world, the edge of existence; there are no allies. Find the spider queen and get the final heart!"

With no response and a fierce look Bellum rode Sathia into the distance on his way to the Capella.

Chapter IX
The Capella

With all three hearts now in the hands of Ursus, Bellum had only one more to go before he could be on his way to find Shaman and the Blade of Eternals. As he rode his horse to his destination, thoughts ran through his mind.

What am I supposed to do? I need redemption! I need to clear my name, even though I never committed any of those atrocious "things" I'm accused of doing. If working with Ursus–our eternal enemy, seeker of ultimate power. My name must be cleansed, and my brethren's honor restored.

They rode far and wide until they found what they were looking for, an abandoned camp holding a suspended campfire with two huge pillars inscribed with the ancient language of the Anaiim, an ancient tribe of peaceful forgers.

"What is this?" Bellum said furious at the fact that Ursus kept him in the dark of the inscriptions on the pillars.

"It looks like Anaiim language, Horseman," the watcher explained, "A race of peaceful forgers that lived in the deepest valley separating this desert from the Demented Forest."

"Key word is lived, watcher."

"What do you mean?"

"When my brethren and I last cleansed Creation from pure evil, we annihilated the race, as we had doubts they were selling weapons for the army of Hell. However, we cannot just stand here and weep. We need to find a way to open the doors for the Capella."

Neither Bellum nor his watcher had any idea about how to read Anaiim. That was an ancient language only taught to the members of the Anaiim tribes.

"Friend," a voice called.

Bellum's eyes scanned the area in an attempt to find the source, "Who is this?"

"Don't be alarmed, friend. I am here to help you reach your goal," the mysterious voice replied.

"How do I know that I can trust you?"

"You don't. But let me take you back seven thousand years ago to the time we first met. You were so excited to meet me that you forgot your parents, who stood and watched you run. I remember all the times we fought together, killing evil beasts, cleansing Creation, and you saving my life more times than I could count."

Bellum couldn't believe his ears, "Sathia?"

"I knew you would remember, friend."

"But how?"

"You do know that we Shadow Horses have the ability to communicate with our riders. That's how you can hear me so can *Comedentis.* You can use my senses to see, smell, and examine your surroundings. Do you remember what your mentor taught you?"

"Yes." Bellum answered as he recalled the teachings of his mentor, who happened to be his older brother *Mors.*

"Here, Brother, take this book. It has all the information you will ever need about Sathia and his race of horses," Mors said as he handed Bellum a small manual.

"Thank you, Mors. Though I am not that younger than you, you always have ways to teach me new stuff I haven't heard of. For that you have my gratitude." Bellum smiled as he opened the first page of the manual where Sathia's drawing was done.

The book read,

Shadow Steed is an advanced race of horses capable of running faster using less stamina. They also have the ability of teleportation, telekinesis, and deciphering old languages. The horse is connected to its rider via a spell only known to the steed's original breeder. If the steed is connected to its master, that bond would never be broken until death, for if the rider dies so does the horse and vice versa."

"That's it! I remember now!"

"Remember?"

"Yes, Sathia. Thank you. *Da mihi veram visionem, Da mihi visus. Da potentia omnia cognoscendi facultatem videre ignotum et explicare, praeteritum et futurum."*

Bellum's crest began to shine, so did the crest on Sathia's armor. The Nephilim could understand the Anaiim language now.

"How can I read this when I couldn't figure it out earlier?" he asked.

"That is my ability, friend," Sathia answered, "I told you I am your most trusted."

The inscription said, *That who possesses evil intent shall be destroyed. Only the pure heart can enter, but cannot leave for here is where eternal peace resides.*

Bellum had no pure heart. He had slain thousands, even millions, of beings, led races to extinction through his blade. The watcher had nothing to offer as well as he was a mere temporary being who kept Bellum at bay if the urge ever rose.

"Dii supra meam audiunt vocant, et aperire ostium magnitudinem. Aperire viam ad ultimum malum et auxilium munda creatura a purus odio." The spell wasn't cast from

Bellum or the watcher, but from the mind of Sathia. With it, the Earth shook, and a large door made of gold and bone with foreign inscribed words that said, *Welcome.*

"This is it. Thank you, Sathia." Bellum walked to the door and opened one side. A bright light emerged as the Nephilim and his companions got teleported to the Capella caves.

As Bellum made his way through the Capella caves, he could see nothing but dead corpses with no skin on them, no head, and not a single drop of blood as they were drained to the bone. The ancient species of spiders was known to love the taste of blood, so Bellum could conclude that it was the work of Distepia.

"She is close. I can feel it," Bellum said.

"Yes, Horseman," the watcher replied, "I can sense the fear floating around the area."

Before the watcher's lips uttered the last words, a huge beast blocked the way center room all drenched in blood. Body covered with crystals, the same crystals that the Mole had on his body; it was her, Distepia.

"I am impressed, Horseman. I couldn't imagine a world where I would be in the presence of one of the Four." Distepia marveled at the Horseman's physique.

"This is no place for a compliment, Spider, neither is the time for it! I came for you, and I will finish my job!"

"The Council now sends Horseman assassins! Do they?" Distepia mocked, "How times have changed. From cleansing Creation and saving lives to assassinating allies."

"I was not sent by the Council, filth! An enemy of yours sent me on this mission!"

"I should have known Ursus was behind this. The Council gave me this power, and they have no reason to take it away from me."

"Indeed, Spider! Your heart will be mine to offer for Ursus as payment."

"You are a fool to trust him!"

"You are a bigger fool to think that a lesser being like Ursus could even attempt to kill one of the Four. If he ever tries to betray me, his life along with his power will be mine!"

"Did you think, even for a second, that your so called 'ally' will let you live to see that he completes his end of the bargain? He will see to it that you are dead before your feet touch the floor of his tomb. So don't be so sure, Horseman! Every life has an end."

"If I die, Ursus will never get his hands on all four hearts!"

"Ursus must not get his powers back, Horseman! He always was in search for ultimate power. Isn't that why the Four and the Council condemned him to eternal imprisonment? Or was it because he slaughtered his own kind? I think it's the first option. And judging by the way you look, I am certain you agree, Nephilim. I am the last of the Chosen Ones and the most powerful!"

"If these are the Council's Chosen Ones, I would have preferred to get other beasts! The first three were weak! You are no different than the rest, Distepia!"

"You will not take my heart! You will never take my heart! Ursus shall never regain his power!"

"We shall see!" Bellum held his weapon.

A powerful battle raged between the two beings in the arena. While the Horseman tried to reach his opponent, the Spider transported herself from one place to another faster than he could reach. Bellum grew tired of the running and the chasing, yet he couldn't find a viable method of getting closer to his enemy, close enough to deliver a fatal blow. As the battle stretched beyond his stamina's capabilities, Bellum needed another way.

I cannot keep doing this fight like this. I need another plan. I defeated all the Chosen ones before her with brute strength, yet she is different. Good job, Council fools, you have created a monster. He thought as he stared at *Comedentis*, the blade. He could control its form as he did against the Mole and the worm queen, but *what can help him now? A chain maybe?*

The Nephilim played out every scenario in his mind, and there was only one successful play he could go to. On the other hand, Distepia did not allow Bellum any time to think or even rest to recuperate stamina, but she continued her attacks one after the other until Bellum was able to cut one of her limbs off.

"You will never win, Horseman! I will make sure of that for as long as I live!"

The Nephilim had a smirk on his face as he charged his foe blade held with both hands, now in the shape of a strong thick chain. Bellum swung the chain as hard as he could and had his hit in the spider's face, stunning her for just enough time to allow him to stab her. The Horseman stood there watching the green blood ooze from his enemy's body, much like seeing waterfalls in the forest.

"Stop, Horseman! Ursus must not get his power back!" Distepia begged as she coughed blood.

"I seek the Dragan and redemption, Spider, and Ursus is the only one who knows where he is! If he is to regain his powers, he can take me there! It may be a risk, but it is worth taking!"

"You are a fool, Horseman! Heed my words, boy, Ursus will betray you! You will suffer and everything you love *will* come to an end!"

"Farewell, Spider!"

With those last words of goodbye, Bellum beheaded the Spider Queen and took out the last of the Chosen hearts. As his bloody hands held his prize, Ursus walked in and stood beside him, "This is the last of them, Horseman! You have done well. I am very impressed that you were able to fight off all of them."

"Ursus…The Spider Queen told me stories about you."

"Things? Like what? Now I'm intrigued."

"That you only desire ultimate power in order to wreak havoc and seek revenge on every being responsible for imprisoning you."

"That part is true, Horseman, yet I made you a promise that I would help you reach Dragan. I keep my promises."

"Very well. I know I am going to regret this, but I own up to my deals, too." Bellum said as he threw the last of the hearts to Ursus and watched him feast on it.

Black aura emerged from the ancient one's body as he devoured the last of the hearts with excitement,

"Finally! I am restored!" He exclaimed as his body began to heal so fast.

Bellum took a step back as he watched Ursus gain all his abilities back. With bad thoughts running through his mind, he held his blade tight enough to be able to launch an attack if needed.

"Horseman! I honor my deals. You helped me, so I will do the same. *Princeps tempus traductor spei audite vocem meam vocem. Aperire ostium ad felicem locum, aperire ostium ad terram spei. Auxilium meum socium suum pervenire metam, auxilium ei ad turrim spei*"

The spell tempered with the literal fabric of time and space as a portal began to appear in front of him leading to a place called the Tower of Hope.

"Horseman, this portal will lead you to the tower where Shaman resides. He is the one to help you find Dragan."

"Anything I need to know about this Shaman?" Bellum asked.

"He is the Angel of Despair. He fell from the Creator's army all the way down to Hell, where Satan took him in and gave him all his powers. The Council wasn't very fond of this new situation, so they imprisoned him in the Tower of Hope."

"Ironic…The Angel responsible for despair and sadness imprisoned in a place of hope and happiness."

"It is ironic, Bellum, yet the Council had hopes that they could turn him around and restore his form before he fell from Heaven. That didn't work as you may have concluded. Take this portal before I change my mind."

"This isn't the end, Ursus." Bellum turned his back to the ancient one and headed to use the portal.

"Until next time." Ursus replied, "But heed my words, Horseman, next time we meet, I will not hesitate to raise my blade against you."

"I wouldn't want it any other way, Demon." Bellum smirked as he entered the portal and disappeared.

Chapter X
The Priest and the Oracle

Bellum took a leap of faith trusting Ursus with his life, but as promised, the portal left him standing in front of a marvelous tower made of steel and gold with gargoyles decorating the high roof. Gold highlights bordered the building as well as the entrance. It was magnificent as if some alien being built it. The Nephilim took his first step towards the tower before he was halted.

"Horseman," the watcher said as a look of despair decorated his face, "I don't think we should go in there. Maybe Ursus sent us to the wrong place. What if we get trapped in here?"

"Don't be silly, watcher! I have no time to waste on your nonsense!"

"Ursus is never to be trusted! You heard all the Chosen ones tell you that! Even Raven did so as well! Why do you put so much faith in that Demon!?"

"If that Demon wanted me dead, he would've killed me, watcher! Don't ever question my judgment!"

"You will regret your decision, Horseman! Ursus will be the end of you!"

"He aided me in acquiring new abilities! He was there when every other being turned their backs on me! Do you expect me to betray him? I am one of the Four! We have honor!"

"We shall see what that honor brings you, Nephilim!"

Bellum had no intention of stopping, nor had he the will to surrender. Finding Dragan was his goal and he would complete it whatever the cost was, even if he lived in despair for millennia.

"We go in, or are you scared, watcher?" he asked with a smirk on his face, yet he got no answer from his companion. The only response he got was a hesitant nod. As Bellum entered the tower, he found exactly what he expected–Shaman, the Angel of Despair, trapped in some sort of force field that stunned any being that decided to touch it.

"Horseman!" Shaman said surprised to see he had a visitor.

"Hello, Shaman." Bellum replied as he walked closer to the force field, "Why are you so surprised to see me? Ursus said I'd find you here."

"I do not get many visitors, Nephilim. Since that day the Council imprisoned me, I have been drowning in more despair than I ever thought possible. I still wonder how I'm still sane."

"I was wondering the same thing, Angel. How come I didn't get affected by the stench of hatred and despair while this filth got wrapped up in it?"

"You are immune. You are one of the Four and being a Nephilim allows you some…abilities. This tower has no effect on non-pure beings, and you being not pure Angel nor pure Demon gives you an advantage along with your brethren."

"I am not here for compliments, Shaman. I came because Ursus said you can take me to Dragan."

"Dragan? I cannot take you to him. I have been trapped here for thousands of years. How is it possible that I would know the way?"

Damn that Ursus! Distepia was right! He tricked me. I will kill you, ancient one! Next time we meet, you can bet on it! Bellum thought as he stood looking like a daydreamer.

"Horseman," the Angel yelled to wake him up from his dreams, "I may not know where he is, but I know someone who can help you."

"Not another waste of time! I don't have that much to spare, Angel! Dragan must be stopped as soon as possible!"

"There is no quest. There is no waste of time. The only thing I need from you is to free me. Once I'm out of this cage, I can open a portal and get you where you need to go."

"Very well, Angel! I will free you, and you shall take me to that person! If you ever think of betraying my trust you know the consequences!"

"I know what the punishment is. Look at my status, imprisoned for thousands of years with no one visiting or trying to help."

"Smart one here. How do I get rid of this 'cage' of yours?"

"Yes, Horseman! In order to set me free there are three Soul Beams each in a different zone of the tower! Direct those towards me and you will be able to overload the shield, and I shall be free!"

"Any other beings…lurking around?"

"This tower is completely empty, Nephilim. Behind you on the left pillar, there is a contraption; pick it up and make good use of it."

The item had inscriptions on it similar to that he saw at the edge of the desert before he fought Distepia. "Is this Anaiim?"

"Good eye, friend. This is the Time Crest. As you can see it looks like a boomerang. When you throw it, a portal will be created, but the distance it could cover is so short that it only consists of a few feet. Use it to reach the beams faster and then to teleport back to me."

"This won't take long."

"Horseman!" the priest interrupted, "Beware while using the crest. Its wielder may have…visions."

"Visions? What kind of visions?"

"No one knows. Either from the past or from the future. In both cases, the crest doesn't lie."

"Yeah, old man, as you wish. Hang in there, this won't take long."

As promised, Bellum went from zone to zone and had the soul beams redirected at the cage. However, when he reached the final beam he noticed something different with the time crest; it had become blood red and lost its bright blue shine. Without any notice or warning, the crest disappeared as the mark on the Nephilim's forehead began to glow.

"Bellum, I love you," a tender voice said as the being behind it planted a kiss on his lips.

"I love you, too, but we cannot do this. I am training to become the next in line for a position as one of the Four, and I cannot get distracted. I am so sorry."

Tears filled the eyes of his counterpart as she saw him turn his back and leave. Before he could leave, she ran toward him with a knife in hand and stabbed him in the chest.

"You cannot do this to me! I know we are young, but my love for you is greater than anything you can imagine. We are meant for each other. This is destiny!"

"My destiny is becoming one of the Four!" Bellum yelled as he took the knife out. To his surprise, there was no blood on it; it was like he didn't get injured, like she didn't stab him.

Why do I have this feeling that this is not real? What is happening? *he thought as he turned back to face the other person in the room with him. Everything became clearer, and he could see everything better; the room they were in, the being standing before him, everything.*

"Naia, this is where we part. I will love you forever, but this is a sacred duty I have to fulfill. I promise that nothing will change how I feel about you. Farewell."

"Bellum…"

"My love, I'll be back for you, because I love you forever."

Suddenly, Bellum found himself standing in front of the last soul beam, blade in one hand and the crest in the other. He didn't want to tell the watcher what happened in that moment.

"What are you waiting for, Nephilim? Redirect the final beam. Stop standing there and move your ass!"

Bellum did his job and redirected the last beam and found himself back in the lobby of the tower standing in front of Shaman, who was now free from his prison.

"Thank you, Horseman." The Angel said excited that he was finally free from captivity.

"I said I was going to free you, priest. Now I want to know what the hell is going on."

"The tower that hosts Dragan has a well beneath it with enough tormented souls to use as weapon to destroy Creation."

"I've heard of legends about a well with souls that can grant you infinite power. But don't you have to complete some sort of deal or sacrifice?"

"You are correct. It is called The Pitt. It contains millions of tormented souls with unfinished business in the world of the living, and it is located beneath the Tower of the Gods at the edge of the world. It is where Dragan resides at the moment. He draws his power from the Pitt as he seeks to gain enough to destroy Creation."

"How can Dragan draw power from the souls when all passageways between Heaven and Hell pass through you?"

"When the Council imprisoned me, they took that privilege away. Who knows who's responsible for soul transfers now, but whoever it might be they are close to Dragan?"

"How do I get to the tower?"

"The only being who knows the actual location of the tower is the Oracle. She is all-knowing and has the ability of foresight."

"How do I get to her?"

"Well, since you freed me I shall repay your deed with one of my own." Shaman pointed at an inscribed tile in the center of the lobby. Bellum walked to the tile as Shaman mumbled a spell of his own, "*Dii Creaturae exaudi vocem meam. Sit tua transeat, et ad tua destination salvatorem mundi et finem omnia mala.*"

The spell cast by the priest opened a portal, much like the one Ursus opened back when Bellum defeated the last of the Chosen. However, this one had a clearer path. It leads to an old house covered with sandstone and surrounded by a forest of pine trees. It had blue shutters and a blue entrance door with the name Oracle inscribed.

"She will help you find all your answers, Bellum. Have a safe trip and best of luck against Dragan."

"Farewell, priest. Until I see you again," Bellum replied as he stepped inside the portal. As he took his first step, he found himself standing in the forest his eyes gazing at the beauty that surrounded him.

"Come in," a voice said from inside the house.

Bellum couldn't hear what that voice said because his mind drifted away in the beauty of the scenery. *Where am I? How can such a place exist when everything in the world is being destroyed?*

Without any clear answers, the Nephilim approached the entrance as the door opened, and a young lady appeared. She was as beautiful as the morning sunrise and even more marvelous than the most beautiful sunset. With long sleek silver-blue hair, light grey eyes, closer to white than grey, and the body of an Angel the Oracle greeted the Horseman.

"I said come in, Nephilim, I was expecting you."

"I thought you might be waiting. Sorry I kept you waiting." Bellum stood there confused as she invited him inside, he followed.

"Don't mind that vase, Horseman."

"What va–," Bellum tried to ask as he hit a crystal vase next to where he stood and broke it.

"That vase." She replied with a smirk on her face. "I know why you are here. You seek Dragan."

Bellum stepped forward as he held his blade tight, "He must be stopped! His evil is destroying Creation, and as one of the Four, my job is to preserve peace."

The Oracle pointed at a small glass orb gently placed on a pillow on a small table, "Let us see what the orb would tell. Beware, Nephilim, what the orb says is what is real. Do not doubt it, or you will never get clear visions."

The Horseman had no choice but to believe her for she had all the answers; otherwise, she wouldn't be the oracle. "*Orbis Lumen ostende mihi viam da mihi responsa ignotum et revelare secreta Creationis.*" the Oracle whispered *as* the orb lit and images started playing. The vision saw two beings, unidentifiable, facing each other without any weapons drawn. *Must be allies,* the Nephilim thought.

"Would you serve in Heaven, or rule in Hell?" a female voice asked.

"You can't make me do anything!" another male voice answered. One could feel the fury in this being's voice.

"If I were you, I would not be so sure about that!"

"I am sure! That is my choice! I have none to begin with!"

"Are you?"

"I am the leader of the Creator's army! It's all the motivation I need! As I said I have no choice. Protecting my kind is what I have to do!" the male voice proclaimed.

"There is! I shall ask again! Would you serve in Heaven, or rule in Hell?"

"I tried to destroy the seals to take control! However, the last seal was not broken! Now I must prevent its destruction! With that the Four won't be summoned! My race will not be slaughtered. I will save them all!"

"I see you have already made your choice, Anxo! You shall become Dragan! Go and tell every enemy of mine that the

most powerful being has risen and that he protects the last of the seals!"

With that, the vision ended.

Bellum stood there, motionless, as if his mind dwelled in another dimension of hesitation and fear. Sweat ran down his forehead as his hands shivered reaching his blade, "Anxo…Is…Dragan!"

The oracle couldn't believe her ears, "Anxo? Dragan? How?"

"I do not know how, woman!" Bellum yelled with anger all over his face, "I trusted him! Everyone trusted him! His job is protecting Man, yet he caused their extinction! He will regret the moment he chose power over duty!"

"Horseman," the oracle said with her sweet voice, "I know you seek revenge, but that is not the answer. Do not commit the same mistake he did. If you want to save what's left of Creation, you have to kill Dragan, and only Dragan. For that, you will need the Blade of Eternals."

As the Oracle mentioned the holy blade, *Comedentis* glowed gold with a shade of blood red which surprised the all-knowing being. "You have the blade, but you are missing the artifact that binds it all back together."

"Artifact? Where do I find it?"

"The answer to your future lies within the past. Search the past for a new beginning," she replied as the area became darker and darker. Few moments later, everything disappeared, and Bellum found himself standing in a destroyed forest.

Chapter XI
A Blast from the Past

The Nephilim was confused. "What does she mean with that riddle of hers? How can the past be the answer to my future, or the future? What the hell is she talking about?" he mumbled. This continued until the watcher had enough and attempted to interfere, "What is wrong with you, Horseman?"

The Horseman was in no mood to answer. He had a strange feeling inside his heart, yet he knew this wasn't real. As he stood there for a while, minutes turned into hours and hours to days without any sense of real time. It was like he knew the whole history of the Anaiim through one memory.

She was born in a world of chaos and death, much like Ursus, yet she never had any intention to obtain power. All she wanted was to find love and to live a life full happiness with a husband and a small family.

Life wasn't so easy for her. Her mother gave birth to her when the Four first went on to cleanse Creation from evil. Bellum wasn't one of them at that time. The Four were their first ancestors. Her name was Naia, the youngest of the race known as the Anaiim, a tribe of forgers specialized in the manufacturing weapons for war and defense.

Naia had a very normal childhood. She learned about the prophecy of the Four from her grandfather, as well as forging weapons from her mother. Unlike other races, the working sex amongst the Anaiim was the females. They forged the weapons and armor while the males did research about other races. Naia had a fascination for reading and discovering new abilities; that was how she learned to do magic. Life was peaceful and beautiful in the Anaiim camp, until that fateful day.

No one knew what happened that night, when the first of the Four raided the town of Anaiim after having evidence of treason. Someone tipped the Council about the presence of illegal weapons of mass destruction created by the Anaiim, yet no one knew the information was false. At that time, Bellum was a little kid visiting the town for the first time to get acquainted with the customs and traditions. That was an important step for him on the road to begin his training to become one of the Four one day.

"Mother, what's going on?" Little Bellum asked. "Why is everyone running?"

Before he could get any answer, he found his great grandfather standing in front of him holding Comedentis on his shoulder, "Boy... Go and hide! The Council should never know you were here. Go and hide!"

No hesitation, no confusion, and no second guessing himself, Bellum ran and hid in a tent between the bushes, and to his surprise little girl hid with him inside the tent.

"Hi. I'm Naia."

"I'm Bellum. Hello." Bellum replied. He never felt this way before. It was like the world stood still at the sight of her green eyes. She was beautiful, blonde hair and a body that appeared to be sculpted by an artist.

"What's happening outside?"

"Um...I do not really know. I just got word from Grandpa to run and hide, so I came here. This looked like a good choice. Now, I'm certain I made the right one."

Naia's smile grew even bigger. She had never been complimented in this way, or even spoken to by any of the Anaiim males. They were all occupied with the task of creating new weapons, so she felt very special at that moment. Bellum stared into Naia's eyes for what felt like an eternity.

"You are very beautiful" he mentioned as his face involuntarily approached hers, lips craving hers, and hands demanding the touch of that sculpture-like body.

She blushed as he planted a kiss on her lips; it was their first, but not the last.

Years passed and Bellum was well on his way to becoming one of the Four, yet he required more training. "Naia, I have to leave."

"Bellum, I love you."

"I have to go, my love. More training is required and the Council calls for all of us."

"We have another choice. We can live here together."

"As long as I am one of the Four, there is no safe space we can live in. Everyone will hunt us."

"I see, Bellum, then it's inevitable. You can't become one of them." She stabbed him with a dagger she held hidden on her thigh.

Bellum took the dagger that she used to stab him and molded it into a small souvenir that looked like a necklace.

"Keep this safe, my love. I will be back for it and for you. That I can promise you." He turned around and headed to the door.

The memory was cut short by a familiar voice barking, "Horseman! Wake up! You have been standing in the same place for more than ten days now! Wake up by the name of the Council!"

"Watcher…What happened?"

The servant took a few minutes to explain to the Nephilim that he went into a slumber by some kind of self-hypnosis only to find himself behind on his quest to save what was left of his dignity and soul.

Bellum was zoned out for a long time, yet his determination was never gone. He rode his horse on his way to explore the area he was in, but he wasn't ready for what the forest had in store for him. As he rode, the path in front of him narrowed more and more until he reached an old oak tree where he tied Sathia and tried to light a fire.

"That's not how you do this," a low voice whispered as if the being with that voice was terrified.

"Who hides there? Come out and face one of the Four."

"One of the Four" was the phrase that encouraged that being to come out of hiding. She was a masterpiece, beauty like no other with a silver gown decorated with natural lilies. Bellum couldn't believe his eyes.

What is she doing here? How did she get here? Who is she? He could not figure anything out.

"Let me do that," she said as she carefully took the tools from his hands and lit a small fire. "There you go."

As the girl took to her feet and stood up, a necklace dropped out from her dress. Bellum was shocked. "That necklace…Where did you get that necklace?"

"I got it as a gift years ago. When I was younger."

Bellum fell to his knees with tears filling his eyes, "I am sorry. I am so sorry."

The little girl hugged the Nephilim without even knowing who he was, "It's going to be okay."

"Naia…"

That name triggered violence from the girl, "How do you know my name?" she demanded as she held her daggers ready to strike. Naia waited for no answer and lunged an attack.

"Naia! I will not fight you!"

"That'll make it easier for me to kill you! Who are you! How do you know my name?"

"That necklace…Adamantium…"

That was enough to stop Naia in her tracks and delay her attack for that valuable second, which allowed Bellum to explain himself, "Nine thousand years ago, I crafted that necklace from the dagger you used to stab m—"

"Be...Bellum?" Naia smiled with eyes full of tears, "Is that you?"

"I am so sorry, Naia, I left without any real excuse just to become one of the Four. I left you behind. I didn't mean to. I'm sorry."

"That doesn't matter, my love. What matters is that you kept your promise and came back for me, and this necklace reminded me of that promise." She whispered in his ear as her arms wrap around his head.

Before she had the chance to kiss him, the watcher appeared out of thin air, "Horseman! This is no time for distractions!"

"Know your place, filth! Don't ever interrupt me again! Now, disappear!"

"What is happening?"

The Nephilim didn't even know where to start the story, "I fulfilled my destiny, as you can see, and I became one of the Four along with *Mors, Ila, and Discordia,* yet I always felt something was missing. You were missing. And now a threat holds this dimension and other dimensions hostage. He seeks to destroy Creation."

"Who?"

"Dragan…Anxo the Archangel and leader of Heaven's army. On his path to defend his race from extinction he lost his mind and made some kind of deal and became this abomination. The only way to stop him is a weapon called the Blade of Eternals. Shaman and the Oracle lent me a hand with information. As you can see, *Comedentis* gained some upgrades from the pieces of the blade, yet the Oracle talked about an artifact that binds it all together."

As Bellum kept rumbling about Dragan, the blade, and the end of the world, Naia stood up, held her hands in the shape of a cross and mumbled words inaudible for the beings beside her, *"Per leges deorum, quaenam leges naturae et physica. Ego Naia Anaiim imperio te ut ostendam in te aeternum lamina grauis socium gladium iustitiae et spes."*

The Horseman's blade glowed with an intense red shade as the glued pieces were released from it. In the meantime, Naia was still casting the spell when her necklace began glowing with the same color as the other pieces. The different parts united together.

There it was, the Blade of Eternals.

"How? Naia." Bellum almost swallowed his tongue as he asked his question.

She looked into his big eyes and smiled, "I am the last of the Anaiim, or have you forgotten?" she said, "Our race has the ability to forge weapons from fragments. You needed this blade and I, as a forger, made it for you."

"Why would you help me after what I put you through? After leaving?" Bellum fell to his knees.

Naia knelt next to him and lifted his chin with her tender hands, looked him in the eye, and kissed him, "Because I love you. Now you go get Dragan and save our world."

The watcher seemed pleased with the new acquisition of the blade, but not with the drama. It was time now to face the source of pure evil–Dragan, yet the location to his tower was unknown. Shaman gave the Nephilim some hints about his whereabouts, but he did not provide exact coordinates or location.

Confusion hit hard.

Even if Bellum located his enemy, the question remained. *How will I take the fight to Dragan? What is the strategy to defeat him?* No plan was clear and no strategy visible in the mind of the Nephilim. That case remained until Bellum glanced behind his shoulder to spot Vulgar in a corner.

"Demon."

"Horseman. I couldn't help myself. I was listening to your conversation with that beautiful lady."

"Speak, Demon!" Bellum said with one hand on his sword's handle.

"You seek Dragan and the Tower of Gods. The tower lies at the edge of Creation, where the sky meets the ocean. There you will find the crest of the Four–the same crest imprinted on your forehead."

"The symbol of the Four? What does the symbol have to do with Dragan or the tower?"

"You see, Nephilim, the tower was built over the Pitt, an infinite well that harnesses tormented souls. The souls are created from beings killed in battle and you, Horseman, have killed countless. Dragan is the Four's counterpart and seeks to rule over Creation and the annihilation of any enemy, even the Four."

"He hasn't faced anyone with the power of the Four! His end is near!"

"Don't get ahead of yourself! First get to the tower, and then face him! I will open a portal for you to get there easily. Shaman, Oracle, and Raven will be teleported there as well."

Since Vulgar was as ancient as the Horseman, if not older, he had mastered his magic which allowed him to cast them without reciting the incantations. The portal opened and the tower was right there. Bellum saw his allies standing in front of it waiting for his arrival.

"Farewell, Vulgar." He stepped inside the portal.

Chapter XII
Baffies?

Bellum found himself standing in front of the Tower of Gods along with Shaman, Naia, Oracle, and Raven who were teleported previously by Vulgar. Blade in hand, the Nephilim scanned the area for hostiles, yet nothing appeared to threaten his journey.

"*Comedentis*...this time you will sit on the sidelines." Bellum whispered as he tightened his grip on his comrade, "You had my back for thousands of years, but this is a battle I have to fight without you."

"I understand." The sacred blade sent his thoughts to his master, "I know you will be victorious, but remember that you can use my abilities on any weapon you hold."

"Thank you, friend."

As he was about to take his first step into battle, he felt a hand on his shoulder; it was Naia, "Bellum," she said softly with tears in her eyes, "I promised myself I wouldn't cry, but I cannot help it. You can turn back. You have a choice; we have a choice. Let's just leave, all of us. We can find a place to call home elsewhere."

"Where do you mean elsewhere, my dearest?" the Nephilim asked. "Wherever we go, nothing will be safe for either of us. I came here with one purpose only, and that's defeat Dragan and to restore the balance to Creation. I can't back down now that I am so close to reaching my goal. From all the beings around me I know you will understand my choice the most."

The bystanders couldn't watch the drama anymore as the time for talk was now over and the time for action started.

"Horseman!" Shaman said, "Are you ready to face your greatest enemy? The battle will not be an easy one. Although you are one of the Four, Dragan's powers are close to yours, if not more."

"What can you tell me about the fight? How can I defeat him?"

The oracle stepped forward holding the crystal orb in one hand while placing the other hand on Bellum's crest. The orb began to glow and showed him a vision from the future.

"To fight Dragan, you must be very wary. He has two forms at his disposal, one being his ultimate dragon form and the other his true form. Fight smart, Nephilim, not hard. The strategy for victory lies within the blade you wield."

With that, the vision ended, leaving Bellum with so many questions unanswered. *Guess I have to figure them on my own,* he thought as he walked away from the beings next to him.

"Be careful, Bellum," the Oracle pleaded.

"Good luck, Horseman," Shaman said.

"Give 'em the baffies, mate." Raven laughed.

Naia had no words for her loved one. Instead, she gave him a hug and a kiss on the lips, "Come back to me. Remember your promise." She shrieked as she started crying.

Bellum walked up the stairs of the Tower of Gods where he passed the tile with his mark inscribed. The Horseman approached the entrance at the top of the stairs. He couldn't feel any hostility in the area.

It was quiet! Too quiet!

As he made his way inside the ground floor, all he could see was the remains of dead corpses scattered all around, blood and broken bones everywhere. With no hostiles around him, Bellum made his way to the first floor where, like the floor before, lay countless detached limbs from fallen victims. *This can't be the work of Dragan... Can it? So much brutality! So much hatred!* The Nephilim thought as he walked around to get familiar with the surroundings.

With every step he took, the ground shook more until he stood center of the room.

"We meet again, Horseman!" a distinct voice said. It sounded like the source of that voice was hanging in midair, so Bellum looked up.

"Distepia!" he said when he saw the Spider Queen hanging upside down from the ceiling.

"I see you remember my name. I'm flattered." The Spider Queen hissed.

"Don't be so happy, Spider! The only flattery you're ever getting is to die at the hands of one of the Four, again!" Bellum threatened. "How is it possible you're alive?"

"Dragan salvaged my soul from the Pitt! When he felt all that energy exiting the Pitt, he decided it was more valuable to him to have me as a bodyguard than to see me dead. He infused some of his power into my life energy and transformed me, something the Council would've never done!"

"The Council gave you the power of an ancient god! They helped you!"

"The Council gave us nothing! We were trapped slaves, each in his own world! Is that the life you want to live? Is slavery even a way of life?"

"It had to be done! You were chosen and you sealed your fate when you accepted their offer!"

"That part is true, Horseman, yet it wasn't the life we wanted! We thought we would be free to roam Creation without hurting anyone! Instead, we lost our sanity and became wilder by the minute! Imagine being enclosed with the same walls for ten thousand years! We were content when you held your blade against us; you freed us from this misery, but Dragan gave us what we really desired. He gave us unimaginable power with the freedom to do whatever we please with it!"

"Seems like you've made your choice." Bellum gripped his sword.

"I did! And now it's your time to say goodbye!"

Distepia had the advantage over the Nephilim, for she was attacking from the ceiling while Bellum had no way of reaching her, or so she thought. As the Spider Queen focused on attacking her enemy, she lost track of how she was defeated the first time. Bellum held his blade, now in the form of the chain again; he twirled it around his head and threw it at the Spider Queen. The chain hit the enemy in her heart and, with full force; the Horseman yanked it towards him as he watched the spider fall to the ground face first.

"This will be the second time you die by my blade, Distepia!" Bellum chuckled. "You should feel honored!" he beheaded her.

Bellum made his way up the stairs yet again trying to find Dragan and end him. Every floor he cleansed only contained few skeletons or resurrected dead corpses, that was until he reached the fifth floor. This was different. The floor was a pool of green fluid, not blood.

"What is this?" the watcher asked.

"Who knows, watcher? Doesn't look like blood, but it's definitely strange to see this here."

"We have to get to the bottom of this unless you don't want to face your enemy."

"We don't have much time!"

"Oh, Horseman!" a voice exclaimed from the other side of the room, "No time? I see we have all the time in the world!"

"You! I killed you!"

"Talpa doesn't die this easily! The master provides us with a lot more power than you can imagine, Nephilim!"

"Your so called master uses you as pawns…All of you! He only wants what's best for him and doesn't even give two shits what happens to you!"

"You don't know what you're talking about, Nephilim! The master is supreme and his safety is above all else!"

"I can't wait to see what he does when I kill you, Mole!"

"Enough!"

"You're just not the type to listen to reason, Talpa! Dragan will have your powers and make it his. Even if I don't kill you, he will! You can't trust a being sprung from a deal with some sort of fiend!"

"The one I can't trust is the Council, Nephilim! They gave us what we had years ago and they took it from us just like that!"

"Everything I did was necessary to lead me here, Mole. And slaying Dragan is my destiny!"

"You can always change destiny, Horseman! Look at me! I am alive!"

"Not for long!" The Nephilim gripped his blade and started a soft jog that turned into a sprint.

Talpa was a new being, red body with even larger claws than before. The crystal that once nested his heart had engulfed his whole body, yet the fight felt like it should've ended way sooner than it did. Though the Mole had more strength, his body was weaker; it couldn't handle as much damage. The fight went on for what felt like hours, having both enemies strike each other, Bellum with deep cuts and Talpa with massive lacerations. The battle had to end before the nephilim lost any more blood, so he jumped as high as he could and smashed his blade into his opponent. Talpa was down.

"You see now, Mole? Where your loyalty has brought you?"

"I was loyal to the Council, and they took everything from me! I was loyal to Dragan and the Council took everything from me! Doesn't that prove something to you, Horseman?"

"That comes to show you that you can't double cross the most powerful entity in creation!"

"It was them who double crossed us when they sent you for us!"

"Pledge you allegiance back to the Council, ask for forgiveness, and maybe I'll consider sparing your life!"

"Please! If I do, Dragan will kill me!"

"If you don't I'll kill you! Your choice!"

"Fine! I pledge loyalty to the Council, the most powerful being in creation! I pledge allegiance!"

"Now was that so hard?" Bellum stabbed Talpa and cut his body from top to bottom.

"Horseman! You said you will spare his life!" the watcher said.

"I said I'll consider it, watcher! That is the punishment for everyone who defies the will of the Council!"

"You really have become merciless."

"Mercy is for the weak, filth! Watch your tone when you talk to me, or suffer the same fate!"

"My apologies, Horseman."

"Accepted! Now to finish the job." Bellum and his watcher continued gaining ground up the stairs until they reached the top of the tower.

Chapter XIII
The Final Battle

It was time to face Dragan, yet the Nephilim had no idea of what was waiting for him. He cleaned his blade from the green goo and made his way up the stairs. As he got to the top of the tower, he saw something he didn't imagine was possible. Dragan was not what he expected. Usually a dragon has scales with red eyes, fierce claws, and a huge mouth to breathe fire. This abomination was different, he…it was entirely made of smoke and ash with yellow eyes and real hands. As he approached the abomination he could see that it had something in its hand; it was Alma.

"She mistook me for someone else! She loved him, and he had loved her…before all of this! He chose duty above all and died! Will you choose the same, Horseman? Heaven hunts you! Hell hates you! Live or die, no one cares! Join me, Bellum! Like a mighty sword, I will raise you up! The spoils of a thousand wars shall be yours! Would you serve a corrupt Council, or a Creator who abandons his most faithful? I offer you this, Horseman! Will you serve in Heaven or rule in Hell? It's your choice!" Dragan said with a monotonous voice as smoke escaped his ashy lips.

"I will choose what a coward once did not."

"I ask you again, Nephilim, serve in Heaven or Rule in Hell?"

"Your existence is a threat by itself. If you cease to exist, Creation will be saved and Mankind will be restored."

"Whatever makes you sleep at night, Horseman! Raise your blade and let's finish this!"

"You don't have to ask twice, Demon!"

Mixed thoughts roamed his brain as he prepared himself to battle. Sword to claw, sweat and blood were the result of multiple attempts from Bellum. He was able to inflict sever damage to his enemy. The evil Dragon didn't want the fight to end so easily, let alone get defeated, so he stood up with the power that remained in his body and mumbled inaudible words, *"Ortum meum sociis. Ortum ex cinere et rédime ipsi. Faciem meam hostes et adducam interitum et dolor ad hoc regnum."*

The ground shook and pits of fire took over the battlefield as Onyc and Deathworm stood strong defending Dragan.

"This is bullshit! These guys again?" Bellum said.

"We meet again, Horseman!" Onyc replied, "You see now the power of Dragan?"

"His power is finite! You can't be serious about following him after you've seen the destruction he's capable of!"

"He brought us back! That's reason enough to follow him!"

"You leave me no choice!"

"You didn't, either! The moment you held your blade against us you left us no choice!"

"My blade shall rise against evil, bat! Whether it be you, Dragan, or even the Council! I was always honor bound! I stood tall all those years and now you will feel my vengeance as I take your mortal soul!"

"You still fight us after you've seen what our master can do? So be it, Horseman!"

Fighting the demons together would prove tough even for Bellum, so he tried just dodging attacks as he thought about a game plan. Onyc went with his fire breath while the Worm Queen rattled the very foundation of the ground. The Horseman knew he couldn't keep it up; he was bleeding and running out of stamina. He had no choice but to fight. As he took a glance at Dragan, he could conclude that the fiend was in the process of healing, so he tightened his grip on the holy blade and threw it across the roof toward the Demon Dragon, landing a blow to the torso.

Dragan roared in agony as he got back up to his feet, *"Accipere potestatem retro! Tolle vita sua essentia, et da mihi plena potentia!"* Dragan said. That spell saw Onyc and the Worm Queen fading away as their essence was converted to souls. Bellum couldn't believe his eyes, a being capable of sealing life's essence? So *Comedentis* wasn't the only thing capable of this?

"How did you do that, Dragan!?"

"Horseman! You don't think that only you possess such power, do you? When I made my deal with the devil I gained this new ability, and it deems very useful!"

"You are an abomination!"

"Sticks and stones, Nephilim, sticks and stones! I lived as a mere Angel serving a Creator who had no obvious plan! How can the one who created all of this be at the mercy of a council!? It wasn't right! We have the right to fight for what we believe in!"

"You do, but not dealing with the devil and falling from Heaven!"

"Fall! You really think I've fallen? I have risen, Nephilim! I am now on top of the food chain in this and any other realm!"

"What you are is a traitor!"

Bellum held his blade on his shoulder while Dragan transformed his hands into claws, the same claws he cut off the arms of the second Chosen. *How is that possible? Him getting the powers of the Chosen I killed? Is it the Pitt? Is it the deal he made?* It didn't matter anymore. Dragan must be stopped at all costs. This time, the fight took a different turn. Dragan was able to inflict more and more damage to Bellum, while the Horseman felt overwhelmed by the strength of his opponent.

Bellum fell unconscious.

Although Dragan wanted Bellum dead, he was still honor bound. He would never hit a fallen enemy, so he just stood there watching the Nephilim drown in a pool of his own blood.

"Come back to me. Remember your promise." Naia's words rang in Bellum's head as he saw himself standing with a white gown. His armor was gone, everyone gone, and nothingness remained. Naia's memory; her smile, her touch, her kiss, everything about her felt so real in the space he was in, yet he knew in his heart this wasn't real.

A voice whispered, "Bellum…" and louder, "Bellum…" and even louder as if the one talking was yelling with everything he had, "BELLUM!"

The Nephilim woke up.

"So…" Dragan said impressed by the determination Bellum had shown, "I see you are not the being to surrender. You are amusing."

The Horseman showed no emotion, it was like he was resurrected as a new being, the old Bellum, the heartless eater of souls Nephilim, "*Sancti lamina meam audiunt vocant, ego praecipio tibi commoda mihi tua virtus vincere inimicum et salvatorem mundi.*"

The spell broke the chains of power set by the Council on the youngest of the Four. His appearance was altered to a dark purple shadow, still wearing the red hood, and with long black hair. No warning! An attack was made. Dragan had no time to react and counter the Nephilim's blade as it sliced through his limbs and cut them off.

Dragan was down.

Bellum approached his foe and, without saying a single word, stabbed the dragon in his heart. Screams of agony escaped the mouth of the fallen enemy as he transformed into his original form, Anxo the Archangel. That didn't last for long, as Bellum held the holy blade, now in the form of two holy daggers, and clipped the Angel's wings. Meanwhile, Alma woke up as the battle came to its closing moments. She saw Anxo in a pool of blood reaching for her, "Alma…" he coughed blood, "Help me! Kill him and join me in ruling the world!"

"You have taught me something, Anxo! Sometimes, duty must be cast aside in order to make the right choice! It is not for duty I kill you now!"

"Alma, please!" he begged her to spare his life.

"Reap what you have sown, traitor!" She decapitated her former general.

"Cruciatus servum meum o legiones inferni cruciatus animam suam de corpore eius et furentur eius extremum spiritum" the watcher whispered.

The spell had Bellum on his knees in pain as his soul once again tried to leave his body. He had no idea what was happening when the watcher appeared with a grin on his face, "I will take the last seal, Horseman You had the last ticket for your freedom, but you lost it! You lost it all! Horseman! You should have known it was a one-way ticket! The Council framed you because they knew that you would play executioner and slay everyone to clear your name, and you did! Your job is done and so are you!"

The Nephilim laughed. The watcher was furious as he couldn't find any explanation to the Nephilim's behavior, "What are you laughing about!? Even one of the Four cannot laugh at his own funeral!" he said.

"I am amused, watcher, that you still think you can kill me. I am not laughing at my funeral. I'm laughing at yours."

The events that followed shocked every being in the area, especially the watcher.

"*Nex Sacrementum*!" Alma stabbed Bellum with his own sword. "The death oath is now fulfilled."

However, she wasn't done with the killing. She left *Comedentis* stuck in Bellum's body as she gripped her sword and went after the watcher. No one knew if it was fear or self-defense, or even precognition, but the watcher raised his hands in an attempt to protect himself. It worked, he wasn't dead, but what he didn't account for was that Alma's blade had a different target, the last unbroken seal.

As they watched the seal shatter into small pieces, a look of disbelief took over the watcher's face, "Hellguard bitch! What did you do? No… no… no!! I will kill you! I will slay your guts through your halo! You will die for your actions now!"

The perpetrator had no time to react and grab the kill as he was halted but a hand grabbing his; Bellum stood in Alma's defense.

"Rise up, Horseman! And I shall kill you again. No matter how many times you come back; you will never get the chance to enjoy it! Remember who holds the leash, Bellum."

"I have never forgotten, watcher!" Bellum beheaded his adversary.

Alma stood there in total shock and disbelief. "You knew! You knew what I was going to do here! That's why you spared me!" She approached him.

"No! I didn't want Heaven's honor to die with its last champion. That is why I spared you. You are now the leader of Heaven's army."

Her pupils grew in admiration, yet she couldn't show him how she really felt about him, "Horseman. In our line of work, I can guarantee we will meet again. However, the next time we meet, I will not hesitate to raise my blade against you."

"I wouldn't want it any other way, Alma. Protect your people and be the champion Heaven deserves."

The newly assigned Archangel couldn't believe her ears. One of the Four was being "nice" for a change. "They will never leave you alone! You will be hunted! There will be others…the Holy City…the Council…and…you would wage this war alone?" she asked.

Words didn't leave her lips fully for the Nephilim to give an answer as the sky became black as coal, although it was still daytime, with a shade of blood red aurora, and a big explosion was heard close by. There they were *Mors, Ila, and Discordia.* As Bellum stood looking at his brethren.

He smirked, "No…I'm not alone!

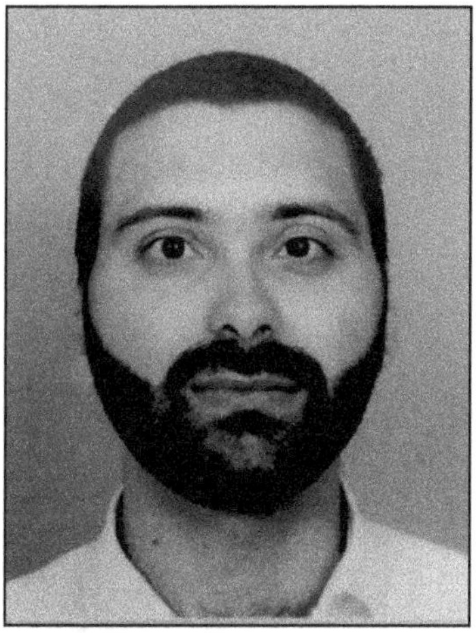

Author George Reaidy was never into writing, yet he loved grabbing a book once in a while and reading it thoroughly as he depicted several plots for the same actions. The same went for Video Games.

His journey with actual writing began in 2015 after a tragic event in his life. It was then that he began writing lyrics and text about a few events in his life that turned into short stories.

George studied Architecture and Interior Design in Lebanon. He was always fascinated with creating something unique without forgetting his love to writing. Bellum was then created and is his first published work.

CPSIA information can be obtained
at www.ICGtesting.com
Printed in the USA
BVHW042008300321
603630BV00015B/997

9 781954 868052